T0245803

Birds of Paradisum

BIRDS OF
PARADISUM

A Novel

STAN LEWIS

NEW YORK

LONDON • NASHVILLE • MELBOURNE • VANCOUVER

Birds of Paradisum

A Novel

© 2024 Stan Lewis

All rights reserved. No portion of this book may be reproduced, stored in a retrieval system, or transmitted in any form or by any means—electronic, mechanical, photocopy, recording, scanning, or other—except for brief quotations in critical reviews or articles, without the prior written permission of the publisher.

Published in New York, New York, by Morgan James Publishing. Morgan James is a trademark of Morgan James, LLC. www.MorganJamesPublishing.com

All Scripture is taken from the New King James Version®. Copyright © 1982 by Thomas Nelson. Used by permission. All rights reserved.

Proudly distributed by Publishers Group West®

A **FREE** ebook edition is available for you or a friend with the purchase of this print book.

_____

CLEARLY SIGN YOUR NAME ABOVE

Instructions to claim your free ebook edition:
1. Visit MorganJamesBOGO.com
2. Sign your name CLEARLY in the space above
3. Complete the form and submit a photo of this entire page
4. You or your friend can download the ebook to your preferred device

ISBN 9781636983776 paperback
ISBN 9781636983783 ebook
Library of Congress Control Number: 2023949786

Cover and Interior Design by:
Chris Treccani
www.3dogcreative.net

Cover Artwork by:
Laura Kitchen

Morgan James is a proud partner of Habitat for Humanity Peninsula and Greater Williamsburg. Partners in building since 2006.

Get involved today! Visit: www.morgan-james-publishing.com/giving-back

DEDICATION

For George, a great storyteller and a courageous
warrior who fought the good fight.

TABLE OF CONTENTS

Acknowledgments

I thank the many people who read, reread, and encouraged me on this project. This has been the most joyful writing project I have ever done, and the most remarkable part has been the collaboration with people who wanted to see this work in print. Phyllis Lofton has been a blessing on several of my projects and a true delight. Laura Kitchen took my crazy ideas for a cover and put them into a beautiful work of art. I prayed for God to bring me the right editor, and He answered that prayer through the stunning work of Kathy Curtis.

Finally, I want to express my appreciation to my family. These remarkable four women have always been a source of strength and encouragement. Kristin has been so patient with my writing, especially when I commandeer the kitchen table with my laptop, books, and reams of paper. My girls have always loved my stories, even when they were bad or I used their favorite stuffed animals to illustrate some ridiculous version of one of their favorite children's stories. Now that they are grown, they still like my stories, and I hope that fun storytelling is something they pass on to their children.

1

Passenger Drop-Off

s the car pulled up to the front of the airport at passenger drop-off, the back passenger door opened. A man emerged from the back after he paid the driver. He dragged his carry-on bags out of the car as he exited. The trunk lid popped up, and he disgorged bag after bag of heavy luggage. Fortunately, someone had abandoned a luggage trolly nearby, so he didn't have to hunt for one.

The man was ready for an adventure. As he shoved the loaded-down cart like Sisyphus pushing the rock uphill, he noticed a shriveled old woman who sat on the sidewalk and leaned against the wall just outside the entrance of the airport ticketing area. The woman made eye contact with him and motioned with her hand for him to come closer. Not wanting to be rude, he reluctantly approached, knowing that this would cost him some spare change and a small amount of time.

The woman wore threadbare and dirty clothes. Her ancient blouse still had hints of royal blue but was now deeply stained and faded, and seven ivory buttons that were cracked and stained adorned the front. However, there were two spots where threads extended forth like little hairs where two buttons once had been but were now missing. Her previously white pants were filthy as if they had not been washed in ages. A blood-red leather belt that she had punched extra holes into held them up, which indicated she had lost a lot of weight over time.

The woman's feet were bare, dirty, gnarled, and chapped, but someone had painted fresh polish on her toenails that represented all the rainbow colors. She had an outer smock that looked like some sort of robe that was matted and pilled but also appeared as if, at one time, it had been a finely embroidered garment.

The ancient leathery face was lively with intelligent eyes, and when she spoke as he approached, her speech was not what he had expected. Rather than a croaky and husky bark as he thought would come out, she had an Australian accent and a lovely soft voice like that of a gentle grandmother.

"Young man, who are you, and where are you going today?"

Perfunctorily, he had already begun to reach into his front pocket for some change when the gentle sound of her greeting surprised him, and she spoke again. "Did you hear me?"

He had not yet removed his hand and replied, "Well, ma'am, my name is Derek, and I am here to catch a flight."

"Obviously, Derek, you are here to catch a flight; only an idiot would assume otherwise. You are at an airport, you have a lorry full of luggage, and you have a look of anticipation on your face, so plainly, you are here to fly somewhere. So now that we have a firm grasp on the obvious, I asked you *where* you were going."

Her sharp wittedness and slight causticness caught him off guard. "Well, if you must know, I am flying to the island of Paradisum."

The elderly woman shifted forward a bit, and with a slight eye roll, a dubious smile appeared at the word "Paradisum." Oh, are you now?" By this time, Derek had retrieved some cash from his pocket. The woman looked at his hand, and the smile vanished. She waspishly snapped, "I am not a common street person! How dare you assume I am out here begging! I don't need your charity!"

Derek saw he had upset the frail woman, for the former pallidity of her checks had vanished, and what remaining blood she had in her emaciated body had risen to her face. "I meant no offense; I was merely wanting to…" His apology was cut short when the angry little crone futilely attempted to stand up. It was clear that age and physical deterioration would not allow that ever to happen again. She fell back to the concrete and against the wall with a thud.

Breathing hard, she demanded, "Young man, come here and sit beside me."

Derek was peeved that he had allowed himself to get caught in this awkward situation. He tried to excuse himself politely and offered, "I really need to get going, I need to…"

With the irresistible persuasion of a grandmother, she demanded, "Young man! I said come here and sit down, and don't make me say it again. I have something to tell you; I will only take a moment of your precious time. Besides, no planes are leaving for a few hours, so you have plenty of time."

Caught and worn down, Derek gave up and came and sat next to the woman. Surprisingly, she didn't smell as bad as he thought she would, and other than her dirty feet and unkept clothing, she seemed as if someone had been taking care of her hygienic needs. When Derek leaned back against the wall to mirror her posture, her outward appearance changed perceptively. She now looked happy and content. He got the feeling that most people had ignored her for so long that any attention was a cool drink of water to her. He felt pleased with himself and secretly hoped that those who walked past would notice his magnanimous humanitarian gesture.

"My name is Allison Bishop; you may have heard of me." Derek had a deadpan look, for he had no idea who she was. "Allison Bishop of the noble house of Bishop!"

"I am sorry, I haven't ever heard of you."

This clearly caused the woman pain, and her shoulders slumped as she slowly responded, "It's fine; very few young people have heard of me or my family. I have a hard time accepting that our once proud family and prestigious name has fallen into ruin. I had ten sisters, and I am the last of the Bishops. None of us had children, and our house will vanish when I am gone."

Derek wanted to get up and walk away. He had no desire to sit and listen to a stranger's family history, no matter how noble it was.

"I know you don't have time for an old woman, so I will make this short. So you say you are flying to the island of Paradisum, is that right?"

Derek nodded in agreement, not wanting to talk for fear of encouraging a long conversation.

"A word of advice, be careful with that and keep an open mind for other options. In my younger days, I worked in this very airport, helping people get to that island, or so I thought. One day, I met a very tall and handsome man and we fell in love, or at least I was in love. He convinced me his only goal was to start an airline to help get people to the island. Little did I know that he only wanted my family's money, and once he got that, we parted ways. Afterwards, I didn't care much for airports, islands, or flying. As I have matured, I no longer think there is some island called Paradisum. Maybe there is, but me personally, I think there are many islands, and it doesn't matter which one you go to. Like I said, keep an open mind about this island business."

Derek could tell there was a hardness in her tone. He listened because her personal story pulled him in, but he felt she probably had some sort of dementia, which made him pity the old woman. Pity or not, Derek still wanted to leave and get on with his trip. As he stood up, he spoke quietly, "I am very sorry for what happened to you, but I just want to have a relaxing trip."

"Sure, sure, go on your trip. All I am saying is don't get all wrapped up in all this island talk. Have a healthy dose of skepticism about you. There may be an island, but probably it is all just good marketing."

"Are you sure I can't give you some money to help you out?"

"I told you, I am not homeless. I have more money than you could imagine." She coughed up a laugh and spoke bitterly, "My money will last longer than I will."

"Allison, it was good talking to you, but I have to go. Thanks for the advice, and have a pleasant day."

And with that, Derek turned to grab the baggage cart and stopped. He reached into his pocket, pulled out the cash, and dropped it on the ground next to the last living representative of the noble house of Bishop. The woman looked at the crumpled money with a sneer on her face like it was something repulsive on the bottom of her foot. Derek never looked back at her but pushed his luggage through the airport doors. Allison Bishop sat there and glared at the money, then looked around to see if anyone was watching. She reached out an ancient hand, picked it up, and stuffed the wadded-up bills into the pocket of her once glorious robe.

2

The Ticket Counter

Derek sped through the airport doors, pushing a luggage cart that strained under the weight of his many bags. He looked more like he was moving rather than just traveling. Excitement filled his steps, for he looked forward to the beautiful white sand and temperate breezes of the tropical island of Paradisum. He had already put out of his mind his encounter with Allison. He had heard much about the island; now, he would experience it firsthand.

First, he needed to purchase a ticket. Like everyone else, he wanted to fly with an airline that catered to customers and gave them a world-class travel experience. Surprisingly, he only saw one airline ticket counter in this massive airport. The "Wide-Open Skies" (some only referred to it by its acronym WOS) airline desk was crowded with people who were like him—weighed down with bags, anxious about where they would sit on the plane, what the flight experience would be like, and if they could get a good seat at a good deal. The desk gleamed with polished surfaces and swarmed with dozens of workers. There were placards, posters, and large television monitors everywhere that advertised their flights to the exotic tropical island of Paradisum.

Derek already downloaded the airline's app that told all about the airline, the destination it served, and all the opulent amenities of the airplane that would depart today. He felt well informed enough to make a sensible purchase. This airline had the reputation of being the biggest and most popular. Everyone who was anyone flew on this airline.

The ticketing area had an inviting feel, and the passenger waiting section was impressive, to say the least. The preboarding space was gigantic, with soft couches and rows of padded seats spread throughout. From the busy bar area, frosted glass doors led to various lounges for business and first-class customers, and oversized leather massage chairs had a line of people that waited to be enveloped once the current occupants finished their turn. The large open area for coach-class passengers buzzed with the excited conversations of those who had already purchased a ticket for today's Wide-Open Skies Flight 1989 to the island. Even with several hours to go before the boarding process began, the place hummed with anticipation.

Beyond the seating area were massive, wide golden doors with sparkling ornate cut glass windows that opened to a broad boarding concourse where people would soon stream in, dragging their bags and pushing loaded-down luggage carts. Thinking that Wide-Open Skies must have a monopoly at this airport, Derek assumed it was the only airline that flew to the island, so he joined the massive queue of people clamoring to get a boarding pass.

As he moved toward the line, he noticed another airline desk off to one side and in the corner of the gathering hall (it was easy to overlook). The ticket counter consisted of a simple wooden desk with a solitary female worker behind it sitting on a stool. The happy young lady had just finished helping the only customer the airline had at the time. The passenger left the ticket counter and passed through a very slender opening (without any bags) into what appeared to be a short, undecorated jetway that ended with a set of stairs that were, in reality, more like a ladder.

The jetway ladder dropped down next to an aircraft of some kind, which Derek had difficulty seeing. Intrigued, and since he had just joined the line, he thought it wouldn't slow him down too much to look around at the other airline desks and the types of aircraft parked outside. He pushed his luggage cart to a set of large windows that looked out over the airfield and the tarmac where the aircraft were parked. As he looked out the window, he laughed.

To one side sat the Wide-Open Skies plane, a massive wide-bodied, four-engine jet with an upper and lower deck, and it was stunning to look at. It looked so impressive that it could have just come from the factory. The aircraft had a beautiful paint scheme, and it absolutely popped in the morning sun. On both sides of the nose of the aircraft, just under the pilot and copilot's side windows, a beautiful Teutonic woman with long flowing robes was painted, with the words *Virgo Spiritus Temporis* underneath her image.

Next to the modern airliner the lone passenger had headed to sat the other airline's plane. It wasn't even a jet but a tiny single-engine prop plane with room for only a few passengers. The aircraft looked ridiculously minuscule next to the jumbo jet, and the entire scene was a humorous spectacle to behold. The humble aircraft had a simple livery and a dull paint scheme, and on the small tail section were the words *Avem de Paradiso* inscribed in small cursive letters. Derek thought the little aircraft looked like it had seen its better days and now needed to be towed to the boneyard.

The solitary customer, a woman who had just exited the jetway, seemed happy to fly with this company, which shocked Derek. When she stepped off the ladder, a man came forward to escort her and help her into the aircraft. Derek could not tell the age of the man, for time seemed to have no bearing on him. It shocked him that this man also appeared to be wearing a pilot's uniform, but he was tall and fit with a well-groomed beard and hair that was longer than what most pilots wear, but on him, it looked perfectly natural and even expected. Most striking, the smile on his face was so incandescently affectionate that one could have assumed that having this woman as a passenger was the greatest pleasure of his life.

Derek couldn't help but laugh aloud at the evolving quaintness on the tarmac below. He thought, *I bet the pilots who fly for Wide-Open Skies aren't helping to load the passengers and the bags on their plane.* In fact, as he glanced back over at the shiny behemoth, an army of ground workers loaded a vast mountain of baggage into the belly of the giant winged titan. As he looked back at the small aircraft, in comparison, it was so narrow and diminutive that there probably was only room for passengers and nothing left for luggage. No ground crew could be seen or even needed, for that matter.

The affair below got more absurd as two massive catering trucks suddenly rolled up to the big plane, and workers rolled dozens of food and drink carts onto a platform that could be elevated to an open door in the aircraft's side. At the exact same moment, Derek looked over and saw the "pilot" of the other aircraft place a small portable cooler in the cockpit area beside his seat. Derek thought this was too good to be true and pulled out his phone to take a few pictures. He mused he might show them to others for a good laugh when he boarded the big plane.

Out of curiosity, he then opened the Wide-Open Skies' app and scrolled to the in-flight meal information. The food page gave a compelling opening statement, "If you worry about what you will eat and drink as much as we do, then your in-flight meals are sure to satisfy." The food and drink options were limitless. One of the highlights of today's flight was that a famous Michelin-starred chef, who went by the name "Gorgon," was on board offering many of his well-known dishes. Derek thought amusedly, *I wonder what type of in-flight "feast" is going to emerge from that cooler?*

While he had been mesmerized by the display of disparity between the two airlines, as if the smaller one would even qualify as an "airline," he thought, another passenger came to the desk and passed through the gate without him noticing. The motion of the passenger walking down the jetway caught Derek's attention, and it mildly stunned him to see another person headed toward the smaller aircraft. He chuckled wickedly to himself, "Boy, the passengers are *really* flooding in now." The traveler was a very elderly man who could barely walk and only haltingly with a cane. As he hobbled to the end of the jetway and up to the ladder, he stopped as if he couldn't decide how to navigate his way around an impossible obstacle. Not realizing it, Derek actually spoke aloud, "Oh yeah, this ought to be good. What are you going to do now, old-timer?"

What happened next left Derek completely stupe-
fied. The pilot ran to the ladder and climbed up to the
man. After greeting him, he effortlessly picked up the
man, climbed the ladder easily, and then carried him
to the waiting aircraft. His strength and agility were
impressive. Derek laughed and then stopped when he
noticed that the elderly gentleman had tears running
down his cheeks. At this sight, Derek felt somewhat
remorseful for his callousness and then reminded himself, "Well, maybe this is all the poor old fellow could
afford." However, if the pilot was embarrassed by having to carry the old man, there was no way of telling.

Derek looked at the aviator and noticed his face was
seemingly ageless and a snapshot of pure joy as if it
were a great honor to have this man on his plane. The
observer wondered if the pilot might have known the
old gentleman by how he attended to and fussed over
him as he gingerly lifted him into an aircraft seat. Even
though Derek felt a bit rueful about his attitude, and as
heartwarming as the scene below was, he quietly continued to chuckle at the preposterous comparison between
the two airlines.

3

The Gate Agent

While he enjoyed his private joke and snickered at the comical scene on the tarmac, Derek looked over and noticed the desk worker from the smaller airline pleasantly smiling at him. Instantly embarrassed and feeling that his joke wasn't so private anymore, he thought he needed to make amends for being so unmannerly. She continued to stare at him to the point that it became awkward. He saw no way out of this humiliating situation except to be a gutless coward and walk away or take his lumps and speak to her. Abashedly, he walked over to the young lady to cover up his previous rudeness, but mostly because he had a genuine curiosity about the bizarre scene on the tarmac below.

"How are you today?" the woman asked as he approached the desk. As a singularly beautiful woman, she had an undistinguishably exotic look as if she said she hailed from any country, and instantly, that would have made sense. Her eyes were lively and engaging, and her voice was most refreshing. Before he could respond politely, the lady said, "My name is Charis, and I hope you will be flying with us today."

Derek stammered, and with a sheepish smirk, he lied, "Well, I haven't decided yet."

"It would be to your benefit to consider our airline for your trip to the Isle of Paradisum. I think once you know more about us, you will conclude that this airline is the only option."

This remark stunned him and he thought that perhaps Charis had lost touch with reality. Then he thought, *No, she's just doing her job and is paid to say such nonsense.* Unable to help himself, he said, "You're kidding, right? I mean, no offense, but look outside the window and compare the two planes." If this remark insulted Charis, she showed no indication.

With a peaceful smile, she responded, "Oh, there is no doubt a big difference between the two carriers; their airplanes are huge, wide-bodied, comfortable, and easy to fly on. We have the one plane and the one pilot, and our aircraft is small, prone to turbulence, and lacks the amenities of the more modern aircraft, but there's more to…"

"Let me stop you before you get too far into your sales pitch. No doubt you are paid to say what you were about to say, but seeing is believing."

"Are you sure you are seeing the whole picture?"

"I've seen enough to know that I have a far better chance of having a good time and even getting to Paradisum, for that matter, in an airplane that doesn't belong in a museum."

"We have never lost a plane or a passenger in all these years of flying."

"Well, you first have to *actually* have passengers before you can lose them." Derek thought this was good-natured kidding, but Charis didn't acknowledge the jab.

"I saw you left the line for a boarding pass for the Wide-Open Skies flight."

"So, you were watching me, huh? I guess there's not much for you to do over here by yourself."

"I have plenty to do, but yes, I do notice people, and my greatest desire is that they would all come and fly with us. Sadly, I know that is not a reality, but one can hope. I also noticed that from your luggage tag, your name is Derek. I'm pleased to meet you, and I hope you will fly with us today."

"Um, thank you." He started to laugh at her last comment but covered it with a coughing spell. "Listen, you seem nice and all that, but I wouldn't get my hopes up too much if I were you about me joining your flight."

"If you have a moment, please let me tell you some things you should consider about your flight to the island today."

He felt he owed her for his earlier rudeness and for the snide comments he had made and shrugged, "Sure, why not? Enlighten me."

"Excellent. The first thing I want to share with you is that our pilot…"

A disturbance across the concourse in the Wide-Open Skies area caused Derek to turn away and stop listening. Charis frowned with disappointment.

4

The Celebrity Pilot

Charis was interrupted by a buzz that worked through the massive gathering crowd that waited to board the big jet. The source of the commotion was the arrival of one of the pilots assigned to fly the giant metal juggernaut. He slowly walked through the crowd; many wanted to meet and speak to this man.

His flying regalia, a bespoke, crisp uniform, gave off an air of confidence and success. A stunningly beautiful Swiss watch hung around one wrist, he wore Italian leather boots that had cost a small fortune, and his uniform was all pulled together by a belt made from some exotic animal skin. He had a tanned face and well-manicured hands, and his jet-black wavy hair had the look of perfection, as if he had just left a salon. This was an impressive man, and he looked like the definition of success.

The Adonis-like pilot enjoyed great popularity among the passengers and many asked for his autograph, took selfies with him on their phones, and pointed him out to other passengers. Others were not so fond of him, but stood off to one side and kept their displeasure to themselves.

The pilot was tall, effortlessly handsome, and had a natural charismatic aura about him. His wife accompanied him, and she was equally as striking, with long blond hair, immaculately expensive clothes, diamond-encrusted jewelry, and magnificent high-heeled shoes (with red soles that made many of the women and even a few of the men jealous). She was far from as extroverted as he was since the crowd energized him, but being around that many people was tedious and draining for her.

The aviator mesmerized most of the crowd, and he engaged the waiting passengers with warm greetings, compliments on their clothing, and gave out handshakes that would have made a seasoned politician envious. He gave a short but super-positive speech about how wonderful the flight would be and how they all deserved to be on this journey. Even Derek got lost in the moment and thought he could listen to this man all day. He was shaken back to the present when the famous pilot enthusiastically waved to Charis as if he knew her. With a brilliantly white smile, he raised his powerfully melodious voice and said, "Hello, Charis! You look blessed and successful today."

"Thank you, I am eternally blessed, Captain Wolfe."

"Well, being blessed, healthy, and prosperous means that you are living your best life now," the handsome pilot jovially teased.

Surprised that this lowly gate agent and the celebrity pilot were somewhat acquainted, Derek asked her, "Do you know that guy?" He had a look of both admiration and curiosity.

"Oh, that's Captain J. Scott Wolfe, and he's one of the Wide-Open Skies pilots. He has quite the following, and it's no wonder because he is extremely likable and has a very charismatic way of motivating others."

"Hey, look, he's coming over!" Derek stated with excitement.

Captain Wolfe slowly threaded his way through the crowd and made his way to what could easily have been a line of demarcation that separated the two airline passenger areas. While the adoring passengers that trailed him suddenly halted as if a minefield lay ahead, he continued with confidence and a familiar comfortableness while he approached Charis. Derek attributed this as a sign of humility and deep character, and he was wide-eyed and mystified that such a famous person would dare be seen on this side of the concourse. The pilot nodded to him as he came to the desk but said nothing, for he had set his sights on Charis.

"Charis, it is so good to see you."

"I wish I could say the same, but you are in the wrong uniform." Her face was grave, and there was a mysterious pain behind her eyes.

"Now, Charis, I know you are disappointed that I am flying for WOS, but I hope you will keep an open mind and be positive about this."

"What is there to be open-minded and positive about?"

"Well, for starters, that a fantastic opportunity has come my way."

"But you once worked for our airline and were on track to be a great representative of what we stand for and believe in."

"I couldn't continue to stay in a holding pattern. Can't you see that I have outgrown this small company, and there is nothing wrong with moving on? Please don't be hurt when I say that. Surely you could see that day was coming."

"I knew you had ambition for an easier life and popularity, but I hoped you would give that up to help grow this airline."

Wolfe took his captain's hat tucked under his arm and laid it on the desk in front of Charis. "I know you, of all people, have given me so much, and seeing me in this uniform has to hurt. But this was an opportunity that I couldn't pass up."

"What could WOS offer you that was so valuable to cause you to turn your back on us?"

"I didn't turn my back on you guys. I hope we can still be friends."

Charis was uncommitted to the "friend" comment.

"Look, I had to make some small compromises to move up and fly for a larger airline; that's how the system works. Here is the blessing, though: I get to help more people this way. And still, I am so grateful to you and the pilot for all you have done for me."

"Our pilot loved and trained you, and now you are working for his competition."

"Are we really in competition, though? We both want the same things—that people would be happy, feel good about themselves, and make it to the island."

Charis responded with zealousness, "That is not what he wants for them; he wants so much more than just some shallow experience in the journey, filled with useless stuff, distracting pleasures, that only ends in pain."

"I am not so sure that it has to end in pain. I have come to understand that the message of this little airline is way too negative. Telling people that they need to make changes, that life sometimes involves suffering, that they have a dark side, and that sacrifice is essential to be truly happy is not the message I can any longer embrace. I seek to inspire people to be the best version of themselves. I choose to take a more positive journey, and working for WOS allows me to do that," Captain Wolfe said with a pained look on his face.

"But, Captain, is that enough? Shouldn't they want more than just having more stuff and believing that success in life should be their life's goal?" The emphasis on the word "captain" was interpreted as a shot across the bow to the aviator.

"You say that with such negativity. There's nothing wrong with having things, yes even nice things (he held up his watch for her to see), wanting to be a success, or even being a *captain*."

"I guess I should call you J. Scott Wolfe like everyone else now rather than Scotty?"

"Well, that's what the advertising guys thought would sound best. I don't care for it, but that's marketing for you."

"It sounds like the name of a lawyer. J. Scott Wolfe, Attorney-at-Law." This made him and Charis smile, and the levity helped break up the tension.

Derek stood there, totally ignored. He felt awkward at the depth of the conversation and about being a bit of a voyeur by listening to an intensely private matter. It also dawned on him how much history these two had between them. He had an impulse to walk out of earshot so they could continue this discussion without him observing, but he was so fascinated by what they were saying that he could not tear himself away. He figured that if these two people wanted privacy, they would have asked for it or walked away. So, he stayed put.

"So, you aren't happy for 'ol Scotty that I am succeeding in life and helping others?"

"No, I am unhappy that you are living a lie, giving people false hope, and endorsing a company that stands for everything you once pledged to stand against."

Clearly, these words distressed him, but he was not an angry or vengeful man. "I hate it when we fight. Look, I have known you a long time, and it makes me sad to argue with you. How many times have we talked about this? Still, you refuse to see my side of things. Since WOS gave me this job and made me the face of their airline, I had hoped for just a little affirmation from you, but nothing. I wanted you to see something positive in my achievements, but you can't or won't; I'm not sure which it is. Don't you see that I have been able to speak to so many more people about how they can live their lives to the fullest, how they can be successful at every station in life, and how to find fulfillment within themselves? Why can't you rejoice for me in my success?" The handsome pilot spoke these words with a clear sense of pleading.

"I guess our definitions of success come from different worlds."

The silence grew more strained as these two former associates regarded each other for what seemed like minutes.

Finally, Charis spoke, "Scotty, I remember when I first met you. You had no interest in custom-tailored suits, watches that cost tens of thousands of dollars, and living in a massive house. You were committed to growing this airline and helping our pilot get people to

Paradisum. But now, you've changed. You have been bought off with trinkets and empty promises, and they are just using you to send a message that our pilot would never send."

At the mention of the pilot, he lit up into the most natural of smiles, and at that moment, it was hard to dislike him. He was sincere, intelligent, and handsome. But, if he thought these assets would melt Charis' hard-line stance against the direction of his life and where he was leading others, then he had underestimated her. While she admired and was concerned for him, she was a towering oak in her convictions and her disdain for the direction his life had turned. He knew deep down that she would not bend, and he admired that about her, but he had chosen to pursue a course that went against everything she stood for.

"Charis, I need to go. I have a plane that I need to preflight. I really do miss working with you."

"I wish you would give up all those silly things and return to work here."

"I'm afraid not. I'm living my best life now, and I don't want to lay that down."

"If that's the heading you want to fly, then I respect your choice. Goodbye, Captain J. Scott Wolfe."

"Goodbye Charis, and I look forward to seeing you on the island."

As Charis watched him walk back to the adoring crowd where his wife waited, sadness filled her face. Derek felt he should not pry into this private affair and pretended not to notice her sorrow, but what he had just witnessed stunned him. To think that this man, who had been a big part of the most recent international PR campaign for Wide-Open Skies, had stood right next to him gave him a thrill. But then, to hear that he got his start in the airline industry at this small-time, minor-league airline was a shocking revelation.

"Charis, I had no idea J. Scott Wolfe once worked for you guys! He's famous. I see his face on all the WOS billboards, and he's great in their commercials. He is literally everywhere promoting their brand."

"We were sad when Scotty drifted away from us." She continued, "I knew his wife also; that's her with him. I hope they have a first-class seat for her, or there could be trouble on that flight."

"Really though, it's hard to be too sad about losing him—I mean, he's flying for the biggest airline there is now. I bet he is raking in the money." Derek was almost daydreaming as he said this.

"Probably so, but that is not what we are in this business for."

Derek rolled his eyes at this comment but kept his thoughts to himself.

She returned to their previous conversation, "Now I think we were discussing the merits of flying on our airline."

With a casual but dismissive wave, Derek spoke, "Hey, I don't want to be rude, but from where I stand, there doesn't seem to be any merits of flying with you guys compared to them." He gestured with both arms extended towards the Wide-Open Skies area when he said "them." He turned to look at the broad gleaming jetway gates and the comfortable seating area of the other airline's passenger reception, which teamed with people anxious to get on board. He turned back to face Charis with an incredulous sneer and asked, "Do you honestly think this small-time venture can compete with the likes of this?"

Charis paused, leaned across the desk a bit, and whispered, "We not only compete with them, but we also far exceed them."

Nonplused at what seemed like an incredibly stupid or deranged statement, Derek responded sarcastically, "Lady, either you're crazy, or you don't know what a real airline is all about. I mean, seriously, you have a small ugly plane, one gate agent (no offense), and a pilot who looks happy to have anyone fly with him." In a low tone, Derek paused and wondered aloud, "He must not be very good if he's not a captain at a major airline like theirs."

With the slight insult of the pilot's credentials, the pleasant face of Charis changed. The smile vanished, and her look caused a shiver of fear to run up Derek's neck. He had the weirdest sense that he had come close to saying something that could have cost him dearly, but he had no idea what that price would have been. Transfixed by her basilisk-like stare, he felt he would never be cheerful again when her smile disappeared.

Charis spoke slowly and deliberately, stern-faced, and with a measured and forceful tone, "We have the best pilot in the industry, and you would be fortunate to fly with him." Her eyes were moist and glistened, and slowly, a smile crept back to her lovely face. Derek felt like the sun had gradually emerged after a terrible storm, and when her radiance returned, he relaxed. Strange enough, rather than repulsing him, Charis' reaction made him want to know more about the pilot.

"Hey, sorry, OK, so you guys have a good pilot, I meant no…"

But before he could finish his flimsy apology, Charis brought him up short, "No, he's not just any pilot, he's not just a good pilot, he's the best pilot that there is—end of story." The smile returned, but Derek perceived that beneath that smile lay a subterranean ferocity that he would be unwise to arouse. He decided to tread lightly with her, for she seemed as if she had the power to shake the very tectonic plates of the earth itself with her defense of the pilot.

"Well, let me ask you, what makes him 'the best there is?' " and with this, Derek made an open gesture with his hand to show a bit of contrition.

"Now that really is the right question, isn't it? First of all, he…"

5

The Gambler

nother commotion interrupted Charis and drew Derek's attention away. He observed two Wide-Open Skies gate agents escorting a somewhat unwilling, if not slightly unruly, passenger to the waiting plane. While the agents looked pleasant, from their size and mannerisms, they were clearly on a mission and were all business. Their "mission" had a singular focus; retrieve the loud and antagonistic little man and escort him to the aircraft. He had been gambling his time away in Vanitas, the glamorous casino next door to the airport.

The Wide-Open Skies company built the establishment for the entertainment and convenience of customers who didn't want to spend their time in the airport shops and food court. Evidently, the poor man had lost track of time and angrily displayed his unhappiness at being fetched and taken away from his expensive entertainment.

With a raised voice, he objected to his treatment, "Unhand me, I can walk by myself! Why do I have to leave at this very moment? I thought I would have had more time before the flight." He continued to protest, "I demand to be put on standby so I can catch a later flight!" Despite his grumbling, the agents continued to shepherd him to the gate. "This is an outrage, and I will make sure that management hears about my mistreatment!"

The volume of the man's voice increased as he grew more agitated. Soon, he pled with his custodians and made quite an uncomfortable scene for the other passengers, "Please, can't I have a few more moments here in the airport? I haven't finished my shopping in the duty-free zone, and there are some items that I want to pick up before we leave." Undeterred, they continued to escort him arm and arm (almost frog-marching him to the plane).

Derek overheard one of the agents say, "We're sorry, Bertrand, but this is the flight you're scheduled to be on, and our job is to make sure you are in your seat when it takes off."

The angry little man unleashed a torrent of abuse, "Tosh! I don't think there is such a place as this silly Paradisum. You are just going to take our money, get us up in the air, and let us all get drunk while you fly around in circles." The fellow slurred his words, and it was evident he had stayed too long at the casino bar.

Not able to bargain for a release from his captors, Bertrand angrily and defiantly yelled, "Seriously! I have heard of these types of flights. They go to no place in particular, and then the buffoon of a pilot concocts some story as to why we couldn't make it to that mythical island. It's a scam, I tell you, and I'm not falling for it!"

The growing hint of panic in his educated English accent was evident. To Derek and almost everyone else, it seemed that he had been drinking to medicate some irrational fear of flying. To reinforce this perception, one of the escorting agents turned to look back at the gawking crowd and lifted a cupped hand to his open mouth in a mock display of chugging a bottle of alcohol. Laughter broke out all over the concourse at the antics of the agent. Bertrand thought the crowd was laughing at him, adding to his annoyance.

As they marched him forward like a guilty man being hauled off to the gallows, the two agents reassured him, "Bertrand, we are on your side; it's just time for you to go."

Even in his slightly inebriated state, the man rejected their pandering. He dug his heels in, making the two men halt. "Don't you know who I am? I am a famous philosopher and lecturer. I have written more books than you two cretins have read in your miserable and unimportant lives. I have argued compellingly that this island is just a ridiculous fantasy. It is a fictional construction of a bunch of thickheaded dolts who need to believe in some placid paradise to assure themselves that they have a place to go on holiday to escape the mundaneness of their meaningless existence!"

Bertrand pulled free and held up a finger to his two captors, and then he quoted a line from a poem or perhaps something he had just made up. "Give me the storms and tempest of a deck of cards and the roulette wheel rather than the dead calm of an airplane seat to an imaginary paradise. Banish me from the floor of Vanitas when you will, but first let me have a roll of the dice, for to gamble is the essence of life and death."

"That's beautiful, but we must still get you to your seat. Believe it or not, you are headed to the island in just a short while."

The alcohol hadn't dulled his intellectualism or his ability to articulate his beliefs. "For you to even talk about the island as real is to reinforce it as an imaginary product of ignorant fools and shameless opportunists looking to make a shilling or two off of the gullible masses and those uneducated dullards who refuse to embrace enlightenment and reason."

The agents nodded politely and got him moving again. They took him through the large doors and into the broad concourse area that led to the jetway and then to the Wide-Open Skies aircraft.

Once more, he stopped them to give them a lecture. His voice was elevated several octaves as if yelling louder could make them abandon their assignment.

"The two of you are only exercising your power over a weaker creature. You think that because you are stronger, I must submit to you. I will not submit! I have power also, power that you know nothing about!" The two overlords looked around as if waiting for lightning to strike and then grabbed the poor man and got him moving again.

As they wrestled him forward, Bertrand grew more shrill and screamed hysterically. "This notion of flying to an island was an absurdity and a clever cheat with no basis in reality!"

"Remember, Bertrand, you paid to be on this flight, and we are only helping you keep your appointment," one of the agents said flatly, apparently getting bored with this situation.

"There is no need to remind me that I have paid to be on this flight, but now that I think of it, I don't want to go. I want my money back. Now let me go! It's a fool's paradise, I tell you! You will never convince me that…" His words were silenced as they escorted him through the aircraft boarding door.

The man's anger and certainty that the flight would go nowhere interested Derek and he tried to use humor to deflect his thoughts. "Wow, he's a live wire, that one. I guess some folks just can't hold their liquor." He looked at Charis, thinking she would share his joke about the drunken intellectual, but she remained silent. He continued his commentary, "Boy, once those airline agents get their hooks in you, they're keen to get you on their plane, huh?" He half seriously asked the question while he glanced at Charis.

Gravely, she said, "Oh, they do hate losing loyal customers and go to great lengths to make sure every seat is full when they take off." There was sadness in her voice, but he attributed it to her just being a bit jealous of the success and efficiency of Wide-Open Skies.

Still, what Derek had witnessed unnerved him. Sure, the little man was intoxicated, but he still seemed adequately lucid enough to express his opinions and even his fears. More than that, he was clearly a brilliant person who had gone to great lengths to disprove the idea of there being an island. His insatiable curiosity kicked in, and his mind wandered. He pondered just what it was that would drive a person of such education and intellectuality to be so irrational about flying and even denying there was an island. While he was not a suspicious man, Derek cataloged this incident as an oddity that he didn't have a sufficient explanation for.

"Let me finish telling you about our pilot."

Derek slightly jumped at these words and noticed that Charis' voice had the effect of snapping him out of a daydream. "Oh yes, please continue," said Derek with bland sincerity.

Charis proceeded enthusiastically, "First of all, no one knows more about flying than our pilot does; why you could practically say that he wrote the book on it. It's miraculous what he can do when flying through rough weather. No storm ever bothers him. Even if the passengers are terrified, they know everything will be alright when they look up at him and see his calm demeanor." Charis beamed as she talked about the pilot. At this point, she lowered her voice, and with a childlike smile and in a hushed tone, said, "Some passengers have even called him a 'storm whisperer.'"

Derek scrunched up his face and looked at her with skeptical eyes. "What in the world does that mean—he can speak to the storms?" he sputtered.

Charis nodded her head up and down without saying a word. Now, he was concerned that he was talking to someone who was psychologically disturbed, and the airline was either a sham or a circus.

He thought, *No wonder this airline is so insignificant; look at the type of wackos they hire.* Curiosity or not, the thought of this as wasted time and a pointless conversation grew stronger. He decided to walk over to the Wide-Open Skies passenger area and enjoy what little time he had left on the ground.

Maybe Derek hoped to get one last parting shot in before he left, or he just wanted to put the woman in her place, so he retorted sarcastically, "Oh, so he can control the weather, huh? It sounds like the passengers who reported those things were pretty liquored up and didn't know if they were in a storm or still sitting on the ground." Derek steered clear of insulting the pilot again; he didn't want to experience the wrath of Charis a second time.

Patiently, Charis replied, "Well, actually, those were some of our first and most dedicated customers who gave that report. Besides, with what is served on the flight, there is no way for anyone to get intoxicated."

This statement piqued Derek's interest in their in-flight meal and beverage service. For a good laugh, he was about to ask what they served on the flight when there was another interruption from the Wide-Open Skies passenger area.

6

The Singer

If the arrival of the celebrity pilot earlier had caused a stir, then that was tame compared to the hurricane of excitement that happened next. A young lady with a large entourage of attendants and security people entered the Wide-Open Skies passenger reception area. Derek instantly recognized her as a megastar. He had a thrill of excitement at the possibility of flying on the same big machine as her. He stood in the same concourse as a world-famous singer at the zenith of her entertainment career. Tall and with a natural earthly attractiveness, she stood out from everyone.

The beautiful diva was fabulously wealthy, instantly recognizable, and commanded massive crowds of followers at her sold-out shows. Millions of people literally focused on every aspect of her life and career. Every time she had a new boyfriend, it commanded worldwide news. When she published new songs and albums, her fans went insane with anticipation for their release. Derek found it hard to envision sharing the same rarified air with a more famous person.

Although she had a casual look with jeans and a red sweatshirt, everything about her screamed that she embodied the pinnacle of human achievement. From the moment she walked in, she ruled the room, and there was a fearlessness about her as she sauntered through the crowd. Her confidence was not unexpected since her security detail had the reputation of easily keeping unruly fans at bay. The people in the passenger area became unhinged with excitement. They pressed in towards her for a glimpse of arguably the world's most important and famous person.

An overly enthusiastic gate agent pushed through the crowd, and surprisingly, he had a microphone in his hand. "Passengers flying on Wide-Open Skies, today we have the special honor to have a true celebrity on our flight! It is the experience of a lifetime to be sharing the same flight with someone of such cultural importance and imminent beauty. Evermore will the passengers of this flight be talking about their journey to the island of Paradisum."

The agent attempted to be as eloquent as possible, as if trying to impress the singer, but instead, his stiff and awkward presentation was overdone and his words made people cringe. His careful phrasing avoided the use of archaic language like "Ladies and Gentlemen" or even referring to the singer by pronouns or gender. Cultured people saw those things as taboo and accepted as the folklore and cultural nonsense of a bygone era of ignorance.

"This remarkable person needs no introduction and is famous the world over, but I would like to speak now about a special event that will take place on today's Wide-Open Skies flight to the island of Paradisum!" The people were breathless with anticipation of what would be announced. "There will be a brief concert just after midnight during the flight. So, if you are a lover of great music, then those who are in the first-class cabin will have a private audience with…"

Something bizarre happened just as the agent was about to say her name. The pilot from the small airline walked into the concourse and headed in the direction of the vending area. Wherever he walked, the lights in that part of the room seemed to grow a little brighter. The gate agent, still talking into the microphone, sounded as if he spoke in a gibberish language and was completely incomprehensible. Derek watched a slow-motion phenomenon unfold.

The people became silent and slowly turned away from the famous entertainer and gazed at the young pilot (or old pilot, for it was impossible to tell his age). Some had looks of admiration, others curiosity. Still, a few looked with stares of purest hatred. Regardless of their expression, every person in that concourse eventually looked at him—even the musician's entourage stopped attending to her and instead were transfixed on him. It was as if some intrinsic autonomic response was triggered simultaneously in everyone. This universal reaction seemed instinctual, unconscious, and uncontrollable, and caused every person to stare at the pilot. The man was overwhelmingly inescapable, and his presence captured the entire concourse of people.

The singer forgot herself and also looked at the pilot. To the crowed, her aura vanished as if she had suddenly been erased from existence. She seemed diminished and plain to Derek and everyone else in the concourse. Compared to the pilot, she was now common, easily overlooked, and anonymous, as if she had never accomplished anything of any true significance in her life. She was now just an ordinary person in a great crowd of ordinary and anonymous people.

Secretly, the woman had longed to meet the pilot and sing for him, for even she had heard of him. But her voice would not rise, and her lips would not part for a song for him. Her fear of the crowd around her kept her silent. As much as she admired this person of such universal magnetism, she also worried how any gesture of affection or loyalty to him might affect her career if she serenaded such a polarizing person, so she remained mute and uncommitted.

With a drink and snack in each of his gloved hands, the aviator walked back to the jetway that led to his aircraft and disappeared. The moment he was out of view, it was as if the power had suddenly returned after a prolonged blackout, and everything that usually made noise sprang back to life. The agent who had been speaking made sense again. The crowd once more fawned over the singer, and her attendants once again pushed people back as they crowded in to touch what they thought was a real person.

The flattering and toady agent concluded his remarks and the singer and her attendants made their way through a large door reserved for high-profile passengers. The crowd was left breathless from the experience. For his part, Derek now strangely wondered if he could ever look again at the singer with as much admiration as before. This brief episode with the pilot changed his view of what he thought was reality and dumped fuel on the embers of his curiosity.

A familiar voice sounded a long way off, "Do you still doubt me when I tell you that he's special and the best there is?" The captivating and soothing sound had a stimulating effect. Derek slowly associated a name with the beautiful sound and realized the voice belonged to a woman who stood next to him.

"Charis?" He spoke thickly and mumbled while he tried to regain his composure, "That was an odd experience." Confident the person next to him was Charis, it comforted him. "When, um, the woman, the singer—

gosh, I have forgotten her name! Anyways, when she came in the room, I thought it was the greatest moment of my life, but when that pilot guy walked through, I completely forgot she even existed."

He realized that he had not been in a trance or some lethargic stupor but rather the opposite. The experience was so palpable and real that his brain was overwhelmed by the event and attempted to process the moment. "Just what is it about this guy? I mean, he strolls into the room for a snack, and everyone has a moment there."

Charis offered, "Well, I hope you get to meet him, for there is no one else like him."

Derek's brain worked furiously now. He felt a growing fearfulness of this man as if he had hidden psychological powers or could look into one's mind and read their thoughts.

Attempting to change the subject and put the pilot out of his mind, he came up with a rather insipid question to ask of Charis. Casually, he asked, "Wouldn't it be great to be in that first-class cabin when she starts singing?" The mysterious moment passed, and he returned to his old self.

Charis walked around the desk, and with a thoughtful glance, she answered his question cryptically, "I'm not so sure it would be worth it."

A bit taken aback by this, he questioned Charis with raised eyebrows, "What, are you crazy? She's a world-famous singer, and getting tickets for her concerts is *suuuper* expensive; I know I've tried. This would be free, and you might get to meet or even sit next to her on the flight!"

Charis drummed her fingers on the desk like a teacher about to give a pupil a bad grade. When she spoke, her words were solemn, "Derek, there is only one person in this entire airport that you need to be concerned with meeting, and that is our pilot."

Derek rolled his eyes and said, "If you say so." His attempt at sounding nonchalant sounded insincere even to his own ears. His irritation with the friendly gate agent increased. She seemed so naïve about what was important in life and the experiences that mattered. Yet, he also thought she worked for a hopeless cause, which made him pity her.

So, now he felt it was his turn to school Charis. He liked her despite her obvious flaws. He hoped to talk some sense into her and he took on the role of teacher with a condescending look. "Charis, listen to me. You have to admit that that Wide-Open Skies has its act together. It's a first-rate operation. Look at their reception area compared to your company's. Then consider this: they have big, comfortable planes, celebrity pilots, free concerts, and amenities galore. Have you ever checked out their food and drink options?" Derek pulled out his phone, opened the WOS app, and clicked on the heading for food and entertainment entitled "Panem et Circenses."

He leaned across the counter to show Charis the screen. "Sooooo, in the main cabin on tonight's fight, they are serving a pan-fried Kronenbourg-infused foie gras with caramelized dates from Saudi Arabia; there is the option of Chateaubriand or Chilean sea bass for a main course; and a lemon-infused sorbet for a palate cleanser. Then, for dessert, you have a choice of Timun black pepper ice cream or a Valrhona dark chocolate tart smothered with whipped cream. Plus—free cocktails and wine! Now that's just in coach class! Can you imagine what they are eating in business and first class?

"Oh, and one more thing, it is all prepared by a Michelin-starred chef who is also on the flight and will sign copies of his world-renowned cookbook. Yes, I know he's not known to be the nicest guy, and he has a very foul mouth, but the man can cook, and that covers a multitude of social sins."

Charis almost seemed bored but smiled patiently and said, "There is more to flying than food, drink, and entertainment."

Derek had enough of these childish attempts by Charis to compare two completely mismatched airlines to each other and snapped, "Oh, I guess there will be a fine-dining experience on your flight tonight? I saw the 'food cart' or what everyone else calls an ice chest that was loaded on the plane."

She casually responded, "Yes, the pilot will serve his passengers with a very simple meal of a loaf of bread and a bit of wine."

His mouth dropped open, but then he thought what she had said was just a joke. He said, "I guess for dessert they'll pass around a candy bar, and everyone gets to have a bite." Derek chuckled at his own attempt at humor, but the serious look on Charis' face told him she was serious, and he stopped laughing.

"What? Oh, you have got to be pulling my leg, that's it—bread and wine? What's the point? You guys should just have the passengers bring their own food. Charis, I don't want to sound critical, but this little puddle-jumper service needs to ramp up its game if you want to attract any real customers. Not having any real meal options is just bad customer service, if you ask me."

Charis gave him a look that suggested she knew something he did not and then informed him, "Well, we have been flying for a long time, and our customers have had no complaints once their flight is over. In fact, our after-flight reviews are solid five stars with no exceptions."

Derek shook his head in disbelief and resumed wondering why he had wasted his time with this poor, deluded person and that he should just walk over to the other airline ticket desk, pay his fare for a seat, and get it over with.

But before he could make his way over, his curiosity again got the best of him. Sarcastically, he asked, "OK, what is the cost of this 'five-star' experience?" He held up his hands and made the air quotes sign when he came to the words, "five-star."

7

The Gate Agents

Charis started to tell Derek the cost when incredibly another interruption happened. Derek felt someone tap him on the shoulder. He turned around and saw two smiling professional people looking at him. They were gate representatives for Wide-Open Skies and asked if they might have a private word with him. One was a female and the other a male, and while they were attractive people, they were a bit repulsive in an undefinable way. He assumed this repugnance came from a perceptible arrogance in their demeanor, but he dismissed it as a bit of overacting on their part as professionals.

Their form-fitting clothing had a provocative style, which gave off an air of seductiveness. The woman dressed in all black except for a blood-red shirt under her jacket. The man wore all brown: a brown suit, brown shirt, brown tie, and brown shoes. His hair matched his clothing as if designed that way. The reps reminded Derek of something primal and foreboding, but he couldn't bring any particular image to mind. He dismissed the thought as an overreaction brought on by the weirdness of this day's events.

When Derek stepped away from Charis, he felt a chill as if he had stepped from a warm house with a cheerful fire and outside into a blizzard. As the two airline representatives spoke, the frigidity increased. The female spoke first, "You're Derek, right?"

Slightly taken aback by what he thought was a cheap parlor trick, he coolly snapped, "Yes, I am. How did you know?"

She replied with a smug and somewhat flirtatious look, "We have been doing this a long time, and we are good at getting people to fly with us. We pride ourselves in knowing as much as possible about potential customers, especially high-value customers like yourself."

He felt pretty good about himself and thought his first impression of these two had been a misjudgment. Elated that an established and reputable business such as Wide-Open Skies knew who he was, he relaxed and became more willing to listen. The flattery, like a pleasant and disarming venom, worked its effects on him.

Direct and to the point, the female agent spoke in a saucy voice, "Wouldn't you like to fly on a real airline rather than with this little wing-and-a-prayer outfit?" She didn't wait for an answer but continued to spin her offer, "Not only do we promise to get you to the island, but the in-flight experience will be beyond anything you can imagine."

As she said this, she gave him a wink, moved closer to Derek, and touched his arm with her hand. Her touch ignited a smoldering desire in his imagination, but just as suddenly, some impulse in his mind caused him to withdraw from her touch, and the moment of passion passed.

In an instant, her counterpart sidled up next to him, deftly put his arm around Derek's shoulder, and spoke into his ear in a low and velvetlike voice, "You really are the sort of clientele we are looking for on our airline."

Derek looked a bit puzzled and said, "I am?" He tried to move away to gain some personal space, but the agent clung to him and pressed in again.

"Oh yes, you are a discerning flyer with an obvious sense of refinement in clothing, and you have the look of a man with good sense and taste." He pulled slightly away from the man and looked down at his own clothing. It was true that he was often concerned about how others perceived him and wanted his appearance to be impressive.

He didn't know what to say and lamely remarked, "Well, it is important to look one's best."

The brown besuited agent continued, "I agree, Derek, for the outward fashions with which we clothe ourselves are just a reflection of what is on the inside."

"Then it's settled; you'll fly with us today! Let's go," the female agent commanded. Her aggressiveness had an unappealing and even somewhat repellant impact.

"Now, wait, I haven't made up my mind, but I'm leaning your way. I need a few minutes to think about it."

The male agent's face soured and lost some of its composure, but he quickly recovered, "Ah, you need a bit of an incentive, huh? In that case, today we have a special deal that we are giving to only a select group of people. If you buy a coach-class ticket, I can bump you up to the business-class cabin." With a haughty smile, he whispered, "We want the right sort of people up there, and you seem to fit our profile, if you know what I mean."

For some reason, Derek grew tired and nearly lost the ability to think. Sluggishly, he said, "Now that is a very tempting offer," trying to contemplate this new development, "and one that I probably shouldn't turn down." Though weary, he felt an indecipherable impulse deep inside to slow this process down and think about it carefully. He didn't understand his own hesitancy about this offer because it should have been a simple decision, but his mind was cloudy.

He remembered the interaction with Charis and the intrigue of the experience with the pilot, which gave him a shot of energy and the courage to put the brakes on the sales pitch. "However, I was having a conversation with this nice lady Charis over there, and I think it would only be polite to hear her out before I say yes to your offer."

The response from these two professionals stunned Derek. "Oh, don't be so stupid, Derek! Why would anyone in their right mind listen to a word she has to say? Quit wasting your time talking to that simpleton!" The surprisingly sharp and foul words came from the female agent, and her voice had a deep maliciousness. While the heat wasn't directed at him, he was insulted and uncomfortable, as if this woman had attempted to intimidate or manipulate him into a quick decision.

The woman's vile outburst made Derek feel like he had fallen into a pool of ice water, which gave him a shot of adrenaline and provided a brief moment of clarity. In that instant, the two agents lost their attractiveness and professionalism. A veil was lifted, and now the two appeared ugly and repulsive. Their eyes were black and lifeless, and their voices had a strange hollow quality about them. At that instant, the menacing image he had tried to remember when he first met them popped into his mind, and a sickening wave of nausea came over him. Then a word popped into his mind, *Run!*

Able to think again, he quickly compared these two "suits" and Charis. She was simple, plain spoken, joyful, and, for some strange reason, imminently trustworthy. The anger she displayed earlier had a purity to it like that of an honorable person that defended someone she admired. However, these two spoke words laced with deception and reminded Derek of touching chilled dead flesh. They didn't come across as authentic and trustworthy in the least.

While the two recovered their professional and cultured look, something inside of him screamed a warning to get away from them and return to Charis. She was a real person, and they were imposters. She gave life away the more she spoke, and they were parasites that captured their prey in a web of words and then drained away one's life.

As if some invisible rope pulled him, Derek walked backward and spoke in a detached and shaky voice, "I really want to hear what Charis has to say."

The male rep pursued and, with a tone of urgency, offered, "Actually, sir, I think we have a seat in first class that we can offer you if that helps make up your mind. Don't forget we have a short concert for the elite passengers in that compartment. Just come with us to our ticket counter and…"

He stopped mid-sentence, and rising on his toes and extending his neck upward, looked beyond Derek toward Charis. Both representatives' faces simultaneously turned to rage and horror at what they saw. They dropped their heads and backed away like threatened beasts terrified of an advancing apex predator. Slowly, they withdrew towards the safety of the Wide-Open Skies ticket counter.

Derek noticed he was drenched with sweat and felt a deep fatigue as if he had been in an unseen wrestling match. He mopped his sweaty face with the sleeve of his jacket and then looked at his hands, which shook. He needed something to drink, for his mouth was parched. He was glad they were gone, and life flowed through him again.

Time came to a standstill, and even though it was moving again, he hadn't caught up with it and felt sluggish and nearly immobile, as if he was wrapped tightly with cords. This encounter had the opposite effect of what had happened to him when the pilot walked through the concourse. Then he had felt invigorated, and his brain synapses fired like crazy, but now he felt like he was coming out from under anesthesia.

His mind tried to comprehend what had just happened, and then he remembered that the airline reps were terrified of something behind him. Slowly, he looked around to see what might have caused them to react like insects when a light was turned on. Finally, he saw the pilot looked at the two retreating operatives. His face radiated with fierceness but not in an out-of-control way with lividness; instead, it was majestically ferocious.

The pilot's eyes were dark brown pools that seemed like they could easily contain all of eternity. He had the look of a skilled and deadly warrior, and his dark hair didn't entirely cover some sort of scarring on his forehead near the hairline. However, the marks on his face didn't detract from his looks, but they made him appear powerful and even strangely approachable.

The room was alive with electricity at his presence, and Derek thought of the earlier claim of him being a "storm whisperer." Seeing him now, he thought that if this man had a mind to do it, he could easily call down a tempest from the four winds with dreadful clouds crackling with savage lightning.

The pilot turned and walked back down the jetway to his waiting aircraft. Derek felt deeply disappointed, and he noticed a feeling of intense emptiness as the man departed from the room. He stumbled back towards the ticket counter, where Charis stood patiently, smiling at him. This last interaction left him exhausted and confused about what to do.

When he came to the airport this morning, he wanted to go on a trip to the Isle of Paradisum, but now it seemed like there was some secretive battle for passengers between these two competitive carriers. If that were the case, then Derek admired the smaller airline's tenacity because they indeed appeared like the underdog.

But despite his growing fondness for the pilot and Charis, he knew he would soon have to decide on a carrier, and he couldn't let sentimentality override reason. Derek had a newfound admiration for Charis and was utterly fascinated by the intrigue surrounding the pilot. However, all he wanted was an easy flight, a good experience during the trip, to be with nice and interesting people, and to check off a few of his bucket list items in the process.

Every time Derek did a quick pros and cons appraisal of the situation, he came up with the same result. Other than getting him to the island, the small airline wasn't able to meet any of his other desires. It only provided basic, no-frills flying on a spartan airplane that offered no amenities whatsoever. Heck, for that matter, he didn't know if the little plane even had a restroom. At that thought, he chuckled to himself.

He believed that purchasing a ticket would be a simple exercise of making the most sensible choice and hopping on a plane. What he had encountered had been more of an ordeal than he had bargained for, and it had left him drained and needing time to think. Even so, if he were honest, his mind was pretty much made up for a while.

However, he first wanted to satisfy his insatiable curiosity for some unknowable reason before he pulled the trigger. He hated the Wide-Open Skies people and thought they were weird and creepy, but the small airline was just that, a small and insignificant operation that was overmatched and outclassed. It saddened him to look at the situation with such a harsh calculus, but so goes life.

Derek stopped a few feet from the desk and sort of waved at Charis. He said, "Maybe we can finish our talk later. Right now, I need to take a walk."

He turned and headed down the concourse, and Charis called after him, "I sincerely hope you think about the things I said, and please come back later so I can finish telling you the other benefits of flying with us."

As he walked, Derek's mind was a tangle of questions. True, the smaller airline had an extraordinary magnetism. Its simplicity, humility, and Charis and the pilot made him want to run and jump into the small plane that instant. Strangely, that small plane seemed like an ark of true adventure. On the other hand, Wide-Open Skies offered to put him in first class, give him the flight experience of a lifetime, and had all the promise of a hassle-free flight.

Flying away on the big plane was the obvious choice. Everything about that airline oozed with luxury and ease and appealed to his heart's desires; the modern aircraft offered spaciousness and comfort, and the passenger waiting area was inviting and broad. Even the giant bejeweled jetway doors suggested that this was the best choice. Yet Derek had a nagging doubt that he could not shake about Wide-Open Skies and what lay behind the glamor of this dazzling corporate monstrosity. So, he walked away to clear his head.

8

The Author

As he strolled slowly down the concourse, Derek noticed the standard places to eat, buy duty-free goods, and purchase souvenirs. However, the one place that stood out and beckoned to him was a bookshop. He thought it might be good to pick up something to read for the long flight, so he walked in. A crowd gathered at the back of the store, and most people were in a knot around a small kiosk with a man that stood behind it. Beside the booth stood a life-sized cutout of that same man. The effigy depicted him smiling, arms crossed, and looking smart and engaging.

Derek approached the back of the crowd and could hear the man talking, "…in the competitive world of aviation, there are many airlines. Most of the smarter and more sophisticated entities that provide service to the Isle of Paradisum, some years ago, at my urging and based on my expert knowledge and extensive years of research, decided to merge into what is now called Wide-Open Skies.

"Some stubborn holdouts still insist that their airline is the only way to get to Paradisum. Most of them have seen the light and at least provide code-share recognition or are in merger talks with WOS. After all, why shouldn't they merge? They are basically the same, providing the same basic service and flying to the same place—just taking different routes to get there. It is silly for them not to combine their resources and efforts. All that does is weaken the industry, dilute everyone's market share, and foster a hostile environment of competition that benefits no one in the end."

The man, clearly an author, was delivering a snippet of the material from the book he was promoting. Drawn in by what little he had heard of the presentation, Derek continued to listen. He reached over and picked up a copy of the author's book from a large stack next to the life-size display.

Two prices were listed: one for the book itself and a higher price for an autographed copy. The cover art was a photo similar to the promotional display. It was of the author with a smug but intelligent look on his face. The title was *Coexistence or Competition? The Emerging Need for the Merging of Modern Airlines and the*

Unprofitability of the Archaic Model of Airline Distinctiveness by Dr. J. Martov. Derek thought the title was boringly academic and sounded more like the title of a PhD dissertation.

Still, the man made some compelling points about the futility and silliness of a bunch of small airlines that claimed they were the best way to get to the island destination. As Derek casually listened, he turned to the book's flyleaf, where the author's bio was explained. He might not have been good at coming up with exciting titles, but his qualifications as an expert were impressive on paper.

According to the write-up, the author had written a string of books on the airline industry. He was a much sought-after lecturer and often consulted for the government on the unification of airlines and how to handle the holdouts that refused to embrace the wisdom of merging and recognizing the value of the other airlines. He did not lack education, for he had many degrees and fellowships from the most prestigious business and aviation management schools.

Derek paid little attention while the man talked, but one statement, that he only caught mid-sentence, fascinated him because of his experiences that day. "...my preference would be that there remain only one overarching organization for the management of the airlines. The most optimum situation would be for the government to merge these companies into one conglomerate. One could call it a forced merger of the airlines." Derek thought of what that would do to the little airline Charis worked for.

Derek paused to listen a bit more, and the author continued, "Certainly, under this arrangement, the authorities would be tolerant and allow the different carriers to retain their identity while also demanding that they work together and recognize the value and offerings of each other. Naturally, those who refuse to coexist must be put out of business because of their inflexibility and narrow-mindedness. Any resistance would be seen as hostility towards the others and damaging to the industry."

Now getting bored, Derek turned to head to the exit when something the author said caught his attention. The man paused and looked up to the ceiling as if in deep thought and then asked, "Aren't they all going to the same location? So, what does it matter which brand of airline people fly as long as there is central control and oversight?

"I understand that some airlines are for a wealthier clientele, others are more budget-minded, and others are for the more adventuresome souls. Still, they ought to all be under one central management group. What I have been advocating is a true revolution in the airline industry. We must eliminate these private small ventures and adopt a model that brings parity and equality to the industry."

Derek thought the last comments sounded slightly off-script and out of place. He felt like the man was trying to slip in some secret agenda. Dr. Martov continued, "I particularly like the broad approach of the Wide-Open Skies model. It would be an excellent centralized managing partner for any smaller airline that should be compelled to merge into this wonderful collective. Having this sort of consolidated governance would be good for all fellow travelers." The small group politely clapped at the end of this sentence.

From the crowd, a young Asian man with a slight foreign accent blurted out an awkward question, "Dr. Martov, don't you serve on the board of directors for Wide-Open Skies, and wouldn't it benefit your company financially to devour the other airlines?"

The author, clearly very polished at handling crowds and familiar with tough questions, casually replied, "Yes, I have a seat on their board, but that doesn't mean that what I am saying doesn't make good economic sense, young man. My life's work is very important, and often, when there is an essential movement in society, a few architects must guide the movement from the top. I have offered my assistance.

"Furthermore, I am aware of the ridiculous rumor that the Wide-Open Skies group wants a monopoly on this particular route so that we would have complete and total control over access to the island. This is, to be blunt, preposterous and irresponsible fearmongering. The Wide-Open Skies company has very responsible corporate values, and our ultimate goal is to bring fairness and equality to the airline industry."

Undeterred by the bloated answer, the young man came right back with a much more pointed follow-up question, "But isn't it true that you have publicly called for the abolishment of at least one airline because they refuse to submit to the Wide-Open Skies demand for a merger and that they also stop claiming to be the best and only way to fly to Paradisum?"

The author's unflappable polish was beginning to wear thin, and with a hint of red rising in his face, he responded, "No one has the right to claim they are the only way to that island, and they should be put out of business for their intolerance of other airlines! If we are to have a blessed revolution in our industry, the airlines must unite under one benevolent banner of equality! There must be a withering away of the state of exclusivity and the emergence of collectivism and unification."

The man pounded his fist on the table before him while he made these comments. When he finished, his breathing was labored. As his presence of mind returned, he realized that his temper had become ungoverned. Angrily, he plopped down on a stool, still breathing hard as he stared at the ground like a bull about to charge.

Stubbornly, the young man stood his ground, "Well, I happen to believe that there is only one airline that can get you to the island. I have met their pilot…" But his comment was cut short when, with the nod of the author's head, a couple of men who wore security uniforms appeared out of nowhere and from opposite directions.

One of them snarled, "You again!" They roughly grabbed him by an arm and manhandled him away from the bookstore and into a windowless door across the concourse hall. Derek and the other customers stood there and gawked at the scene, and wondered what would prompt such a display of anger and police state tactics.

Dr. Martov picked up a water bottle and took a long swig. After he regained his cool, he calmly smiled and said to the crowd, "I must apologize for the rudeness of that irritating person. There are still those backward souls who simply will not believe that the airline they chose to associate with is not the only option!"

He stopped again with a dramatic pause and a deep sigh. He confessed, "Actually, I don't blame that poor man, for he has no doubt been deceived into believing such tales by that tiny and insignificant airline that is right next to the Wide-Open Skies gate; I think you are all well aware of which one I am talking about." Many in line nodded in acknowledgment, and some even rolled their eyes to show their contempt.

He continued, "Their gate agent, which they only have one, by the way, indicates how pathetic they are. She is a mindless zealot with a singular focus on talking about how great their pilot is. I guess he'd have to be great to fly a death trap like the one sitting on the tarmac out there. Besides, that pilot is stubborn and reckless, and even if he were that good of a pilot, I would still never want to fly with him. I couldn't abide his intolerant claims of exclusivity."

The author dropped his head and wrung his hands, "I am so sorry about all of this unpleasantness over something that should be all about the experience of the journey. I don't think I will take any more open questions, but I will happily sign some books."

Derek did have an inquiry, but he didn't want to worsen a prickly situation or get carted away by tough-looking security guys to some dark back room. He decided to buy a book for the autograph and casually ask his question while the writer signed the inscription. He paid for the autographed copy and joined those seeking his signature. The line moved quickly since most people remembered the man's warning about taking no more questions, and instead, they decided to engage only in polite small talk with the man.

As he reached the front of the line, Derek handed the book to the author seated at a table and politely suggested, "Dr. Martov, would you please sign it to Derek?"

He opened the book, looked down, and started writing on one of the first few pages. Taking a slight risk at that moment, Derek asked, "I saw the pilot for the airline that is next to the Wide-Open Skies passenger area, and he's an interesting man. You don't seem to have a very high opinion of him. Why is that?" Derek thought he had done an excellent job of couching it as a seemingly harmless question.

The author paused, looked up into a smiling face, and decided it was just a minor indiscretion brought on by the man being starstruck by meeting a famous writer.

He put down his pen and gathered his thoughts. "Listen carefully; it's not that I dislike the man because I truly admire him. The problem is he is too dogmatic, and on top of that, as I mentioned, he's reckless. He will not work with the other airlines or cooperate with them whatsoever. He goes against wind and tide to venture out in all types of risky weather, never deviates from his course no matter what storms are in his path, and insists that his passengers do everything he says without exception. Furthermore, his baggage policy alone borders on absurdity and is an embarrassment in our industry."

He stopped and put on a more genteel face, "Perhaps I was a bit harsh towards him because he is a marvelous pilot, and granted, he could fly for any airline, but he stubbornly stays with that small operation. Of course, it is a little understandable since he is the one who founded the airline in the first place. I guess he just can't admit that it will never be a broad-minded success like airlines such as Wide-Open Skies. On the other hand, you must hand it to him; his little company continues to fly. I attribute that to the strength of his character and passion, but it is clear that he has taken his airline about as far as it can go. So now, um…"

The writer looked down at the name he had written in the book, "Oh yes, Derek, so, here's the hard truth. This business is cutthroat and is no place for do-gooders and those who believe in fairy tales. Your pilot out there needs to modernize and change with the times if he wants to survive. If he asked me for my counsel, I would advise him to drop all this distinctiveness mumbo jumbo and merge…"

He continued to talk, and while he was nauseatingly impressed with his own words, he had a genuine admiration for the pilot of the smaller airline. However, since he was also a paid spokesman for WOS, he kept his remarks on a more critical note.

As he continued with his diatribe, he promised there would be one last bit of commentary on the pilot, "To close the subject on this man, as I said, while he may be a legend in the industry, that is not enough. Furthermore, I don't believe for a second the miraculous reports of his flying prowess. That's all just clever marketing, which is probably the real secret for their survival to this point."

Although he had promised only one last comment, his arrogance and unawareness of others drove him to continue the seemingly eternal monologue. "The truth is the model that he has based his airline on is from the beginning of the industry and is now hopelessly outdated. Seriously, to think that only one small airline is capable of getting all the people to Paradisum is, as we say in Russian, gluppy or silly."

For the first time, Derek noticed a hint of a Slavic accent. "Just walk over and take a look at their aircraft! It's ancient, and I've seen crop dusters that can carry more passengers! We live in a modern age, and if some small airline can't keep up with the demands of modernity, they need to go out of business and make room for those who will give the people what they want."

Derek reached for the book and felt awkward about the amount of time the author had devoted to his query. Self-conscious that the others were growing annoyed with him, he attempted to move on. As he reached for the book and prepared to offer thanks for his time and the autograph, the writer placed his hand on the book. Derek interpreted this as an obvious power play and a nonverbal cue that they were not done.

"I hope you are not seriously thinking about flying with that farce of an airline—that would be a big mistake. Wide-Open Skies is a much better option, and I'm not just saying that because I am on their board of directors. You look like an intelligent, sophisticated, and thoughtful person, and WOS is the airline of choice for discerning flyers. If you like, I could call a friend, and we could get you on today's flight, no problem."

He had the feeling that things were about to get strange again. Why would this man offer to do this for some random stranger? The randomness of this offer perplexed him, and he thought there was some conspiracy to keep him away from the other airline. In an instant, he dismissed this thought as pure whimsy. "Thank you for your kind offer, but a gate agent already promised me a first-class seat on today's Wide-Open Skies flight."

The writer's eyes widened at this revelation, and he jumped up and exclaimed, "Well, you would have to be a fool to pass that up! You need to get your ticket now and head on into the first-class passenger lounge—it's called The Silver Mine Lounge, and it's fantastic."

Dr. Martov dropped his voice and cupped his hand to his mouth as he leaned towards Derek, "You will like the lounge because they have great food and drinks, comfortable seating, and most of all, you won't have to mingle with 'the great unwashed masses' out in the coach passenger waiting area." He winked at the end of the comment, which made Derek slightly uncomfortable, as if a well-respected person had just told an inappropriate joke and you didn't know if you should laugh or not.

The arrogant writer hadn't noticed that he had created an awkward situation with his classism faux pas, so he continued, "The bottom line is that no matter what airline you fly, it's the same destination. It's the journey or the experience that is what's truly important, and WOS will give you the best experience. I know I would rather fly in style and comfort with fashionable people eating good food, drinking fine drinks, and having a good time rather than risk my life on some harrowing and uncomfortable wild ride while barnstorming on some uncivilized and backward airline that caters only to a bunch of witless peasants."

The more he talked, the more uncouth and condescending he became. It became apparent that for all his talk of equality and the collective good, he was a person who craved an elevated and comfortable life and wanted to be with the class that had the right sort of people.

While Derek looked for a polite way to exit, something the pompous man had said troubled him. The question stuck in his mind, "Since we are all going to the same place, what does it matter which way we choose to get there?" Despite the man's blather, he thought he made a reasonable point that he should file away and ask Charis if he ever ran into her again.

9

The Warrior

While the author chattered on, many of the other customers grew annoyed, but the self-absorbed intellectual continued to spew his tasteless drivel. Some who had hoped to get an autograph stepped out of line and walked away. The haughty man hadn't noticed the thinning crowd and that he was now losing book sales.

Suddenly, out of the corner of his eye, Derek saw movement from the same windowless door the young Asian man was taken through. The ominous portal swung open, and that same young man was ejected back through it as if shoved from behind. The two security men followed him out with stern looks on their faces and spoke in what could only be interpreted as a low and menacing manner. While not pronounced, it was clear that the man had a slight limp as he walked slowly away from the door. He headed back in the direction where the two airline gates were located.

Derek reached down and grabbed the book. He quickly looked at the boorish man and said, "Thank you for the autograph and an informative discussion." He walked briskly away because he wanted to escape the vainglorious buffoon who incredibly continued to talk. He mostly left because something told him to catch up to the guy who hobbled away. Sheer curiosity drove him to go after the man.

Dr. Martov called to him as he exited the bookstore and said, "Tell them in the first-class lounge that you know me, and they will introduce you to the flight crew. I know one of the pilots who is famous…" and with that, his words were lost in the din of the concourse chatter.

As Derek pursued the other man, he thought it strange that the interaction with Dr. Martov had produced the opposite effect instead of deterring him from learning more about the other airline. He couldn't see the significant threat from this small airline to a giant monster of a company like Wide-Open Skies.

Everyone he had encountered who was associated with WOS (except for the celebrity pilot), from the two ghoulish gate agents to the egotistical author, were either terrified of or hateful towards this small operation with only one gate agent, one pilot, and one plane. If the small company was as bad as these people said, it should have been out of business years ago. However, it seemed like the company had been around forever and would be around for the foreseeable future, much to the dismay of Wide-Open Skies and their representatives.

Something didn't add up about the entire situation, and this made him even more curious. He couldn't shake the feeling he was being lied to. The dark idea that an unseen someone was pulling the strings of some grand conspiracy took root in his mind. Suddenly he shook his head and said, "Oh, come on, get it together, Derek." He tried to dismiss these thoughts as the product of an overactive imagination and a strange and stressful day. "Don't get pulled into the petty politics of the airline industry. And for goodness sake, stop believing in fairy tales and conspiracy theories!"

At that moment, he caught up to the young man who walked slowly, nursing a limp. He glanced sideways at him and said, "Tough day, huh?"

Derek expected a scowl and the man to unload on him about the unfairness of his harsh treatment, but instead the response came as a pleasant shock. He smiled with a broad, toothy grin that was spectacularly cheerful but was also marred by a trickle of blood that ran out of one corner of his mouth. "This day is nothing; they just don't want the truth to come out about what is really going on. If you think this is bad," and he pointed to his swelling lower lip, "then you should hear what all the pilot of the other airline has been through."

Derek skeptically wondered if he had made a mistake talking with the man. He now thought he could be dealing with an insane person, for no one would laugh off this sort of treatment unless they enjoyed pain or were just looking for attention. The mention of the pilot kept him engaged, for he wanted to know more about that man.

Derek continued with the conversation, against his better judgment, which told him not to take the dialog any deeper and to walk away. However, his honest curiosity dragged him deeper in. "Wait a second, just what did you mean by that remark about the treatment the pilot has received?"

The other man stopped walking and wore a pleased look like a fisherman who had just felt a tug at the end of his line. He answered, "Oh, my friend, you can't imagine the pain that man has been through to keep open the only true and trustworthy route to Paradisum. It is almost inhuman what his competitors have put him through."

This statement shook Derek. Even though he thought this fellow was either melodramatic, delusional, or just a rank troublemaker, he no doubt just had an unfortunate encounter with security. All of this seemed to be associated with his passionate defense of this pilot person. "So, why did they rough you up?"

The man smiled as if the treatment were a badge of honor, "Well, it's not the first time, and it's not the worst that has happened to those of us loyal to the pilot. They, the WOS, don't take kindly to those who challenge their attempts to monopolize this air route. Any spreading of the truth of the real situation is met with a severe response. I think the official stance on it is called pacification by force."

Derek's mouth hung open as he looked at the grinning man who wiped the blood away from his mouth with his shirtsleeve. "That can't be true. This is just two competing airlines fighting for passengers, right?"

"Is that what you really think is going on here?" The question from the stranger hung in the air with a deafening silence between the two men. Like a patient angler, the young man started walking again, letting the befuddled Derek think about what he had just asked. He walked after him in deep thought.

Derek responded from behind as they walked, "Well, I think so, or at least I would have believed that until a few minutes ago when you came out of that room, having been obviously beaten up by those two thugs. Now I don't know what to believe. As far as I know, you are just some unstable agitator who likes to cause trouble."

If Derek had intended to end the conversation through sabotage by making the man angry it hadn't worked. The man just laughed and replied, "Agitator? Well, maybe. Unstable? Definitely not, or at least in my opinion, I'm not unstable."

They stopped walking again. "Look, I am not all that concerned about your opinion of my mental state, but let me ask you a question if you don't mind." Derek nodded his approval, "Have you had any strange experiences since you came here to buy a ticket?"

Derek gave a half laugh and said, "Man, you have no idea; this whole day has been the strangest experience of my life!"

The man didn't want to set the hook yet and introduced himself, "First of all, my name is Xi. Xi Shengmo. Thank you for speaking to me; most people just avoid me as if I am some kook or radical."

Derek gave an uncommitted smirk and replied with only his first name. He didn't want to get in too deep with this guy.

"So, Derek, I bet you keep running into people who think you need to be on the big plane, and they keep telling you that you are stupid or crazy if you don't. It's like there's some concentrated effort to steer you through those broad jetway doors." The smile vanished from the young man's face, and he looked deadpan at Derek.

With a bit of healthy skepticism, Derek replied, "Yeah, so what? That could be explained as overaggressive salesmanship."

Xi nodded his head and admitted, "You're right, but why the big effort to keep you and others away from the other airline, to sabotage the reputation and demean the flying skills of their pilot, and to label anyone who shows any interest in flying with the smaller carrier as imbecilic or a freak?"

Derek could see that he would soon run out of answers if these questions continued, but he offered,

"Well, maybe they're right, and the tiny airline is hopelessly outdated, a sad relic of a bygone era. Maybe the pilot is only fooling himself to think that he can compete with the likes of a massive beast like Wide-Open Skies."

He believed Xi would counter this and use the opposite argument that Dr. Martov used and was surprised when, instead, he changed tactics unexpectedly. "Look, I could give you statistics, evidence, and what I think are irrefutable proofs that the whole Wide-Open Skies company is a sham and there is some shadowy conspiracy behind it all. I could also try to persuade you that the smaller airline is your only hope of getting to the island, but I'm not sure you would buy any of that."

With that statement, Derek thought, *Oh boy, this guy is a lunatic.*

Xi then reached into a pocket and pulled out a badge with his picture on it. To Derek's surprise, it was a Wide-Open Skies employee badge that said "Ground Crew Supervisor" on it. "Yeah, that's right, I used to work for WOS and was completely sold out to their vision of all the airlines becoming one big happy family. I believed the propaganda that all the airlines were essentially the same, going to the same place, and should all have the same corporate values."

Derek held up a hand, stopped Xi, and said, "Wait a minute, you, the guy who just got beat up, was once a supervisor for WOS?"

Xi had his fish on the line, but just barely. "That's right, Derek. I was good at my job, moved up in the company quickly, and was a well-paid disciple of their corporate philosophy."

Derek became profoundly interested but also wary of this man. He wondered, *What if Xi was just a disgruntled former employee who only wanted his pound of flesh for being fired or something?*

As if he knew his thoughts by the look on Derek's face, Xi smiled again and said, "And no, I wasn't fired; I quit."

"Quit? And why would you do that? If you had it so good, why leave a great job?"

Xi responded, "Because I met him, I met the pilot. You see, all of us employees were told that we couldn't associate with him and should stay as far away from him as possible, so I did. You wouldn't believe all the horrible things management said about him and his airline, and I simply accepted it as true. The company policy was that he was a persona non grata, so I avoided him at all costs."

Derek gave Xi his full attention, but it wasn't like the previous experience with the two WOS reps. Then he felt like their venomous words sedated him, but the more Xi spoke, a strange energy surged through Derek, which helped him think and cleared his head.

Xi continued, "Then, one day, I watched one of our birds take off, an aircraft I had just supervised the ground operations for. I looked around and realized I was completely alone, which never happens. Typically, when one of our planes departs, the entire ground crew stands outside and watches because it is an awesome sight. I looked around to see where everyone was, and then I looked over at the tarmac area where the other airline loaded passengers into their small plane. I saw the pilot leaning against his plane, watching our aircraft leave the runway."

With the mention of the pilot, Derek's attention became hyper focused. He wanted to know more about this enigmatic man, and now he hoped he was getting accurate firsthand information. "Strange enough, the pilot didn't seem angry that our plane was packed with people and his was not, but he was, well, sad."

At this point, Derek stopped him and asked, "Wait, you knew he was sad? How? Was he crying or something?"

Xi picked up where he left off, "Yes, I knew he was sad because I could see tears running down his face."

Derek had an odd look on his face, like pity or disgust, but Xi couldn't tell which. As if to address his feelings, Xi said, "Yeah, I, too, just assumed he was sad about how miserable his airline was doing compared to ours. Then he looked at me, and I was truly scared to death. It felt like we were the only two people on the planet—it was very strange. Then he walked towards me, and I wanted to run, but it was like my feet were stuck in the concrete, and I could not move. I was terrified of him, but deep down, I somehow knew that he wasn't coming over to harm me. I also looked around to see who might be watching, and I realized that we were alone on the tarmac.

"When he got close to me, he didn't just look at me; it honestly felt like he was looking inside of me, like I was being X-rayed and nothing was hidden from him. Then he said, 'Xi, my friend, why don't you leave Wide-Open Skies and come and work for me?' It was strange, but as intimidating as he was, I didn't feel like he wanted me to be intimidated, but instead he wanted me to speak freely and honestly. So, I said, 'Sir, why would I ever do that? What could you offer me that WOS hasn't already given me?'

"He smiled, and the more he smiled, the stronger I desired to say 'Yes!' to him even though I had no real reason to do so. Then he told me, 'I can't give you any of the perks and benefits that your present company gives you, but what I can offer you is a chance for your life to count by helping others to get to the island.' I admit I was confused and told him, 'Well, isn't that what I am doing now?' "

The look on Xi's face as he came to this part of his story became one of intense pain. "Derek, what he said next I will never forget. He had stopped smiling, and his words caused a deep fear like I had never felt before. 'No, you are not; tragically, you are helping to get these people to another island, but not Paradisum. It is an island of sadness and not true pleasure. I know this because I own the island of Paradisum, and I have made many houses there for those who allow me to take them there.' "

Xi had set the hook hard, and he had his man fully invested in hearing the end of the story. At this revelation, Derek looked like a man who had been hit with a jolt of electricity. He had never considered even the possibility that there was more than one island. Xi resumed, "I admit I was stunned at his words, but deep down, I knew they were true. I can't explain it; something inside me knew I was hearing the truth for the first time. Then I asked him where these people were flying to, if not Paradisum, and he told me, 'They are going to the island of Tartarus.'

"I couldn't make sense of what he was saying, but there was clarity about his words and searing truth in his eyes. I questioned him more about this because I had met so many pilots and crew, and I believed they were sincere professionals who knew how to fly and navigate.

"He told me, 'They can fly the aircraft and follow a chart to any place on the planet except the Island of Paradisum. They cannot get there because I am the only one who knows the way and is skilled enough to fly there. Your company's leadership has given them charts that have the label Paradisum on an island, but it is not my island; it is another one. That island is a sun-scorched rock with no beaches, no five-star hotels, no tropical breezes, and no birds or animals of any kind; it is just a clever deception that a slick public relations campaign has propped up. What you have worked so hard to accomplish is to perpetuate a lie that has hurt so many people.' Then I had the strangest feeling come over me; I felt guilty and loved at the same time."

"All I have ever heard is that there's only one island," Derek said.

"Yes, I know, that is all that I had ever heard as well, and I worked for an airline."

"This is the craziest thing I have ever heard," Derek responded. The fact that Xi had worked for WOS was the only thing that kept Derek in the conversation. If it was anyone besides a former employee, he would have called them a loon and walked away. "For that to be true, it would take a fairly sophisticated conspiracy to make that happen. We're talking next-level cloak and dagger stuff."

Xi responded with a deadpan voice, "Do you know what makes a convincing puppet show? It's when you can't see the strings."

"How did you know what this guy was feeding you was legit?"

Xi had to wipe away the tears that brimmed in his eyes. "I knew what he was saying was true. I instantly realized that I had been working for a crooked organization that had been deceiving people, and I felt shame and sadness for my part. I looked at him and asked him what I needed to do, and he told me, 'Come and work for me. You can be one of my recruiters who tells people the truth about the island and my airline. If you will do this, then one day, when it is time, I will take you to the island, and I have a house there with your name on it—it is yours.'

"At that moment, I knew I didn't deserve his offer of a new job and a place on the island, but I also knew that if I walked away from this, I would regret it forever. So, I said I would come and work for him, and I have never looked back."

The emotional part of Derek saw a broken man and his story deeply moved him, but the rational part of his brain could not accept it. Derek thought, *That's too quick of a change to be authentic. No one just makes a snap decision to walk away from a good and prosperous life to work for a failing organization with an uncertain future.* He thought, *Either this guy is super impulsive, or there is something he is not telling me.*

He wondered what was left out of the story and his curiosity pushed him to ask an obvious question, "So, just like that (Derek snapped his fingers), you quit your good job and went to work for a guy that you hadn't met until five minutes before? No evidence that what he was saying was true, no investigation of his claims, just jumping off the cliff in the dark?" His question had an accusatory and skeptical tone, but Derek didn't care because he wanted the truth. If this man was a huckster, he wanted no part in his scam.

Xi cocked his head to one side and just nodded in acknowledgment, but then he qualified his nonverbal response, "Yes, and no. Yes, it was a leap, but no, not a leap without evidence."

Derek bored in on Xi's story, thinking it was about to fall apart as he exposed some plot hole in this tall tale. "I don't understand; he didn't give you any evidence that what he was saying was true. How can you say that it wasn't a jump without any proof? If I were going to make that big of a change, you would have to give me more than just a bunch of funny feelings on the inside. I would want concrete and irrefutable proof. It sounds like you either aren't very intelligent, or you were taken in by a con man."

If these words upset Xi, then he never showed it. "I understand, and that's reasonable, but incredibly, the proof had been right before my eyes the whole time, but I had ignored it. Every day, I saw passengers board our plane and secretly watched as passengers boarded his. There was a vast difference between the two groups. Most of our passengers were shallow and concerned about the cares of this life to the point of obsession. Please don't get me wrong. Many were very nice and even sincere in how they lived their lives, but ultimately, they only wanted to have fun on the flight and a nice and easy journey to the island."

Xi looked up thoughtfully and said, "You know, the baggage was what really got me. I guess that only makes sense because all day, every day, I supervised the loading of massive amounts of luggage. You wouldn't believe the types of things that people would drag with them on their trip to the island: silly things, priceless things, shameful things, illegal things, ancient things, religious things, dangerous things, and on and on ad nauseam! The people who travel on Wide-Open Skies like their stuff and don't want to give it up. Here's something else about the baggage: we never checked or restricted anything. Nobody cared what you brought or how much you had. It's not like that where I work now; we have a very strict baggage policy."

At this point, Derek cut his eyes sheepishly towards his own luggage trolley that strained under the weight of all his bags. Subconsciously, he moved just a bit to put himself between Xi and the cart. Then he thought, *So what if I have a lot of bags? A lot of folks have tons of stuff, and that doesn't make them bad people.*

Xi pressed on, "There were days that I frankly couldn't believe our plane could get off the ground being as weighed down as it was with luggage. Then, there were tragic days when I would hear that a plane had crashed because it was overweight. Of course, management would say that it was pilot error or blame it on the weather, but the ground crew knew better. Never once were there any directives from on high to curtail the amount of baggage because it was important to keep the customers happy and unaware of the dangers they were in. As long as they were ignorantly pacified and the company kept growing, that was all that mattered. So, I kept loading the planes and sending them up in the air."

Derek was engrossed in the story, especially after he heard the bit about overloaded aircraft falling from the skies. He also wanted to know the difference between the Wide-Open Skies passengers and those who flew with the pilot. It had to be more than just the amount of baggage. He asked Xi, "You said the other passengers on the small plane were different; what did you mean? Were they weird, unintelligent, or just a bunch of backward people who didn't know how to have a good time?"

Xi laughed. "No, they were normal people and from all different types of backgrounds, but they were, well, different. The best way to describe it is that they had committed themselves to the idea that the pilot was the only one who could get them to Paradisum, and they lived their lives as representatives of him. They were willing to give up anything and go through all sorts of trouble to get his message out about the true way to the island.

"When those people showed up at the airport, they had prepared for the flight through sometimes years of service to him. They weren't concerned about the flight or if they could bring their stuff and any precious comforts with them. Things like in-flight entertainment, food and drinks, dressing up to impress others on the flight, and who was in first class, business class, or coach meant absolutely nothing to these people. They were the happiest people I had ever seen, and I should know. I watched them load that little beat-up airplane every day, and often, when they took off, they were laughing and singing.

"On the other hand, our passengers were usually frightened, concerned about whether their luggage had made it on board with them, what class they were to be seated in, and who they would be seated next to. Those flying with us were usually anxious and even uncertain about making it to the island.

"Sometimes, fights would break out over some of the pettiest things even before they loaded the aircraft. Then, others couldn't have cared less if there even was an island and often went so far as to deny its existence. They were there for the 'experience' of flying and were adamant that the flight would end at the same place they took off. To be honest, that group was usually the angriest and meanest people I had to deal with. They simply had no hope of anything to look forward to at the end of the flight.

"As for the other airline, I never saw one unhappy or dissatisfied customer crawl into that little plane. Those passengers seemed truly grateful to be flying with the pilot. All the while, there was this massive, beautiful monster of an aircraft sitting next to theirs, and it was as if they never gave a nanosecond of thought about switching to our aircraft. So, yes, the evidence was right there, and I had chosen not to consider it. I suppose I just willingly accepted all the disinformation that upper management had put out about the pilot and the people who flew on that airline."

Derek stood there considering these words and doubted that choosing which airline to fly was as simple as he had initially believed. He, too, had seen a difference in the two groups of passengers, but he hadn't considered why. The people boarding the Wide-Open Skies plane were concerned about their stuff, what they wore, and what they would eat and drink. Entertainment and having a good time seemed to be their focus. Those were the things he focused on, which was why he wanted to fly on WOS.

But the two passengers he saw board the other airplane were the opposite. They had no baggage; they made no demands about where they would sit, nor had they inquired about the flight's amenities. Then it hit him square and hard like an unexpected punch, "I would probably fit in better on the big plane than the small plane." The thought bothered him, and he couldn't figure out if he should feel bad about it or just be indifferent.

Xi's words pulled him out of his thoughtfulness, "The day I changed jobs was the best and worst day of my life. When I told him yes, it was like a massive weight lifted off my shoulders, and I felt like a free man. That was the best part. The worst part was when I went to tell my bosses what I was going to do. I thought maybe they would let me put in a two-week notice. Call me naïve, but I thought maybe I'd get a severance package or a going-away party. Instead, they were furious and called me a fool and threatened me; I mean, they physically threatened me if I didn't reconsider."

"Why the violent reaction? That seems extreme for a job change."

"That's what I thought—extreme, too extreme. At first, I thought they felt betrayed or threatened because people in leadership positions like mine never left the company. Honestly, it didn't make sense, but I have never seen my managers so angry. The more they pressured me, the more I understood the real reason for their anger."

"What was it?"

"It was the pilot—the management of WOS, especially upper management, hate him in a way that is unnatural. When I tried to tell the story of my experience with the pilot, they laughed at me and called me gullible and stupid. When I told them my decision was final, things got really hard core. They told me they would ruin my life and bring legal action against me. Then upper management got involved and sent a couple of guys to escort me out of the employee area.

"As they walked me out, they hit and kicked me, and while I was on the ground, I seriously thought they would kill me. Truthfully, I think they would have killed me if the pilot hadn't shown up at the right time. Those guys ran like frightened children when he found me. He picked me up and took me back to his employees' breakroom, and there, a lady named Charis took care of me and attended to my wounds."

"I know Charis, nice girl, but I am not sure she is all there."

"Oh, she's all there. But a word of warning. Don't ever insult the pilot in front of her. Her wrath is spectacular when she is defending him."

"You don't say."

"After I left, my friends I worked with immediately cut me off and refused to speak to me. The people I once worked for and trusted spread rumors and lies about why I was no longer with the company. The WOS security hassled me for no reason when I would come to work at my new job."

"It's hard to believe they could get away with that sort of thing; that should be illegal."

"It should be, but WOS has a lot of power. Honestly, though, it was fine. The worse they treated me, the more I understood that I had made the right choice and that WOS was truly an evil organization."

As Derek listened, he looked like someone who had just learned some deep, dark family secret that had suddenly turned the world upside down. He could not unhear the story Xi had told him and realized his world was not as right-side up as he had always believed it to be.

But then something snapped inside of Derek, for he stepped back from Xi as if he wanted to travel backward in time to that moment where he had not heard these things, back to a time when life was understandable, and the trip to the island was a simple and thoughtless transaction.

Xi perceived the conflict that brewed within Derek and said calmly to the frightened man, "Derek, why don't you talk to the pilot yourself? I would be happy to introduce you to him. What do you say?"

He had secretly wanted this, and now Xi handed it to him. He didn't know what to make of this offer to speak to the pilot. He had seen a glimpse of him and how he affected everyone in the concourse earlier. He also had heard Xi's story and sensed truth in it—or at least Xi believed it was true.

His curiosity became an inescapable gravitational field that drew him toward something he simultaneously both feared and was attracted to. Yes, he wanted to meet the man, but he feared what would happen or what the man would say. Then again, if he walked away, he might never get another chance. Derek pursed his lips and then nodded his head yes.

Xi was ecstatic and pointed to a padded bench along the wall and said, "Wait over there for just a minute, and I will be right back!" With that, he was off in a limping gallop to find the pilot.

10

The CEO

Xi took longer than he should have, as if he had been detained. Derek grew impatient because he wanted to settle this question of which airline to fly once and for all. He also wondered if he was being silly and making more out of this whole thing than he should. *What if he is just an ordinary man like the rest of us? They say you should never meet your heroes because it is always disappointing.* In frustration, he threw up his hands and murmured, "It's just a flight to an island, for goodness sake." Now, his imagination started to run, and he pondered if a con artist took him in with a convincing story.

As he sat there debating with himself about the situation as if from nowhere, he noticed a very tall, handsome man walking towards him with a couple of large burley escorts. He was dressed entirely in white from head to foot, with one exception of color. His clothes were as white as a swan except for the blackest of black silky neckties. His custom-tailored suit comprised of a beautifully fitting jacket with an English cut, trousers with a knife edge of a crease down the front of each leg, and a matching white waistcoat. His shoes were made of supple white leather like they were made from the hide of a baby unicorn. His black silken tie was held in place by a large pin with a head of stone that glimmered with a hue of colors as the light hit it. In truth, it wasn't one stone but a collection of many smaller precious stones in a setting of gold.

Even with his towering size and conspicuous clothing, no one else in the airport noticed him. One might have thought that he wore a cloak in anonymity and walked unseen among the teaming masses, and was only gloriously perceptible to those with whom he wished to interact. To everyone else, he was just a phantom. As he drew closer, the more uncomfortable Derek became. The man didn't simply possess the typical height of a tall person; he loomed large and radiated an imposing presence. He locked eyes with him, exuding a focused intensity.

As the white-suited man walked up to Derek, he felt he should stand up, for he had the countenance of a person of great importance. Even standing, the stranger towered over him. He stopped several feet away and looked down, considering the smaller man. Then he spoke, and Derek couldn't help but listen, for he had the most melodious baritone voice he had ever heard. His voice matched his persona to perfection and sounded exactly what one would have expected it to sound like. More than that, his vocalization was pitch-perfect and undulated like the most seasoned and well-trained thespian.

"You must be the man Derek I have heard so much about today. You gave a couple of my trusted associates the slip when they offered you an incredible deal. You are a hard man to bargain with; I admire that." His eyes twinkled and even though he wore a placid smile, his face was inscrutable and sphinxlike.

"Yes, my name is Derek, and who might you be?"

He bowed his head in a gentlemanly gesture, "I seem to have forgotten my manners; I know your name, but I have not given you mine. I am Mr. Reinhard von Lux-Ferre, the Chief Executive Officer and founder of the Wide-Open Skies airline company." His manners were formal and perfect, and his speech was captivating and reverberated through the air. When he spoke, Derek noticed that his intonation had a musical quality that sounded regal and ancient. His voice carried such power and mysticism that it resonated deep within Derek and felt as though he could sing an enchanting melody capable of captivating anyone with its noble and majestic richness.

"It is very nice to meet you, sir. I really like your airline."

"You like it, so you say, yet you haven't bought a ticket for today's flight. Why might that be, my friend?"

"Well, I've been looking at all the options."

"That is very wise and commendable. My philosophy is it is unwise to limit our appetites, but rather, we should sample all the fruit of the garden before making a choice. You seem to be a man of great wisdom who likes to weigh all the options before he makes an important decision. I hope I can help you make the proper choice today." The sound that came from the lips of the CEO had a soothing and hypnotic effect.

Derek thought, *Now this a trustworthy soul and someone well worth listening to.* But more than hearing him, he seemed like a person Derek could tell his deepest, darkest secrets to, and he would greet him with only understanding and a complete lack of judgementalism.

The voice continued to disarm him as it asked, "What can I do to help clear things up for you and speed you on your way?"

Almost robotic in his response, Derek said, "I just want to go to Paradisum."

Mr. von Lux-Ferre smiled and replied tranquilly, "That is exactly what I want for you also. My greatest pleasure in life would be to see that you go there. Don't you want to walk with me to our ticket counter and let me take care of that for you?"

Derek again found himself in a stupor, but this time, he didn't know if he wanted to fight it. The words gently drew him in. The voice had strength and nobility, and pulsated with wonderment and delicious, mysterious overtones that held the promise of ultimate fulfillment.

"Yes, that sounds like an excellent idea."

Yet Derek stayed seated. He struggled to remember something very important that held him in his seat. He vaguely recalled being told to do something by some-one recently, and it involved staying on the bench, but he could not remember why or who had told him to stay there. Then, a simple thought entered his mind and manifested as more of a picture than a conventional thought—a face. Yes, the face belonged to someone important and powerful. He wore a pilot's uniform. Yes, the pilot of the smaller airline!

He struggled to hold the image in his mind and the specifics about this man, but he did so with great effort. Then he asked, "Before we go, can you tell me what the story is of this pilot from the other airline? Honestly, he is so blasted strange, and I can't get him out of my thoughts."

The CEO fidgeted just a bit as if this wasn't part of his plan and then calmly spoke, "I am one who finds rudeness to be detestable. With that said, it will proba-bly sound very rude of me to talk about my competition, but please know that my words are only meant to pro-vide clarity and not insult. However, let me tell you a tidbit or two about that tragic and sad man, and then we shall walk over and take care of your ticket.

"You see, I have known him a long time; he and I go way back. There was a time in the distant past when we were friends and worked together. If I am honest, and I am always honest, he is the man who first gave me my start in this business. Over time, I saw us as becoming equals, but he refused to see it that way. I finally understood that he was holding me back, and I could no longer grow while under his legalistic thumb. My great sin was that I had the ambition to grow the business, and, yes, it would have meant a bit of a promotion for me, but that would have been only fair. His petulance and jealousy of my better ideas drove us apart."

The large man stopped and dropped his head. "I don't like to tell this story because there are too many bad memories. Truth be told, his father built this airport, and after I parted ways with them and their failing enterprise, I worked tirelessly to build my own airline; it's the roaring success that you see before you—Wide-Open Skies. Even though it was hard to start over, through my superior business acumen and some shrewd corporate practices, I got a foothold in the airport, acquired a gate, built the airline, and now I live only to serve the public. I freely admit that this was not my original idea, but it is one I have improved upon and greatly enhanced."

The CEO, suddenly distracted, issued a command in a somewhat hurried voice, "Derek, let us take this enticing conversation over to our beautiful lounge where we can have more privacy."

"I really need to stay here; I was told to wait on this bench."

The giant man reached over and grabbed Derek by the arm, lifted him up, and steered him toward the Wide-Open Skies lounge. Derek wanted to protest but found the magnetism of the man hard to resist and questioned whether he even wanted to do so.

11

The Pilot

Before the sluggish Derek and the irresistible CEO took many steps, a voice that sounded like thunder boomed the word, "Stop." This marked the first time Derek had heard the pilot speak but even with only one word he became mesmerized. This one utterance completely eclipsed the voice and cultivated speech of the tall man who held him. Derek had previously found Mr. von Lux-Ferre's words beautiful and melodious, but in comparison to the pilot, they now sounded tinny, hollow, and out of tune with reality.

Derek, Mr. von Lux-Ferre, and the two associates instantly froze. From the direction of the concourse where Xi had headed to find his boss, he and the pilot approached. Xi had a menacing look as he eyed the tall man. The pilot exuded an aura of complete control, as if he were the very eye of a hurricane.

He spoke to Mr. von Lux-Ferre, and what he said was not a request but more like a command. "I would like to have a word with Derek, so release your grip on him." Instantly, Derek felt the pressure of the man's grasp relax and was free from the powerful vice and the melodic spell of the large man's words.

Xi could no longer contain himself, for he was spoiling for a fight. "I'm sure you have filled his head with lies to get him on your doomed flight to nowhere!" He looked earnestly at Derek, "You mustn't listen to this wretched viper. I'm sure he forgot to mention that he once worked for our pilot but plotted to take over his company in a secret coup but was discovered and fired for betrayal."

The CEO gave a wicked smile as he looked down on Xi. With words that dripped with malevolence, he said, "Ah, if it isn't Mr. Shengmo, my treacherous former supervisor. I see that you are as troublesome and deranged as ever. My best people have had a devil of a time trying to control you. I admit your meddlesome tactics have cost me many valuable customers, but we have very effective tactics for handling traitors and…"

Xi shot back at him, "I'm well acquainted with your tactics! I just had a couple of your goons try to keep me from getting to my boss! Fortunately, he found me before they could do me any real harm. When they saw him, your little minions took off before they could really go to work on me."

"Why, Mr. Shengmo, you unpleasant little man, whatever do you mean? I would never dream of harming someone. I am just an honest businessman seeking to serve the public. Who knows what actually happened to you, for everyone knows how prone you are to make up wild stories like the amusing one you continue to peddle about the day you left my employment."

"Lies!" Although the giant was easily twice his size, there was no fear in Xi's face, only a bloodthirsty quest for battle. The pilot had a handful of Xi's shirt and held him back.

The large man smiled, put a hand up to his heart, and professed, "It pains me to hear of your trouble today. However, in the interest of peaceful relations between our airlines, I assure you that I will investigate what happened to you today with the greatest priority."

"More lies!" Xi spat.

"Mr. Shengmo, as often as you have run afoul of airport security, I am surprised they haven't issued a shoot-on-sight order for you, seeing that you are such a hopeless nuisance. It would be best if you were more careful with security personnel. You never know when one of those poor men will have had his belly full of your bothersome antics and make a tragic error in judgment. As pestilential as you have been, one could hardly blame them, though." A hungry and malicious look crept onto the mask of Mr. von Lux-Ferre's otherwise serene face.

Mr. von Lux-Ferre desired to continue goading Xi but stopped when a booming voice that shook the floor said, "Enough!" The pilot had spoken, and Mr. von Lux-Ferre instantly stopped talking.

The blood rose into Xi's face, and his fists were clenched as if he were a fighter ready to spring out of his corner swinging at the sound of the bell.

The pilot looked at Xi and softly said, "Xi, you are a great representative of our airline, and I appreciate your fighting spirit, but let me handle this one, would you?"

Xi mumbled, "Yes, sir." Then he added, "But if you want me to…"

The pilot brought him up short with a firm hand on his shoulder and a stern but gentle glance, "Xi! I've got this." Xi dropped his head and stepped back, glaring at the smug and gloating CEO.

"I am here to talk with Derek and extend him an invitation for me to fly him to the island of Paradisum."

"Well, by all means, my dear intrepid aviator." With that, the CEO bent forward in a mock obeisance and flourished with his arm. "Talk to him all that you would like. After that illuminating conversation, you could show him around your stately reception area, then take him out and give him the grand tour of that spacious and glorious wonder of modern aviation that you call an airplane. Maybe he could wash it for you while he is out there. It wouldn't take long, and it could certainly use a good wash and even a new coat of paint. As for enticing him to fly on your airline, perhaps you could tempt him with your in-flight amenities."

The large man turned and addressed Derek, "You, sir, are in for a real treat, for this little airline is famous for their over-the-top hospitality."

He addressed the pilot, "Now remind me again about all the benefits of flying with you. Ah yes, now I remember. As for the entertainment options, your guests can look out the window, or if that gets old, they can look out of another window. Then there is the scrumptious multicourse meal that you serve, and when I say, 'you serve,' I literally mean that you serve it. And by the way, what is on your extensive menu today? Oh, that's right, it's bread! The same menu as yesterday and the same as it will be tomorrow.

"I must agree that your catering service is exceedingly consistent, if not sadly unimaginative. That delicious feast is sure to leave your passengers pushing back from their tray tables, saying, 'Oh no, I couldn't possibly eat another bite.' But then they get to wash it all down with a swallow of wine. You certainly have spared every expense, and you really know how to spoil your customers." The CEO took great pride in this sarcastic performance; even the ordinarily stony-faced associates snickered at his jokes.

The pilot stood silently and allowed Mr. von Lux-Ferre to continue speaking. He made no effort to defend himself or his airline and looked perfectly composed. Xi, on the other hand, was so angry that he appeared as if he could spontaneously combust at any second. Derek could see that the pilot had resumed his grasp on Xi's shirt just in case he decided to launch a sneak attack.

Curiously, though, a faint dislike for Mr. von Lux-Ferre grew in Derek's mind. Maybe the pilot deserved all this hectoring, but it was still difficult to watch an attack on someone who refused to defend themselves. At first, the CEO had all a gentleman's deportment and suave words, but the more he spoke, the less of a gentle-man he seemed to be. Still, Derek thought this conflict was some old unresolved grudge match between these two men. He knew that long-running feuds can some-times bring out the worst in even the best of people. He decided his best course of action was best to reserve judgment as to who the culprit was in this conflict.

The large man continued with his snarky barrage, savoring every second of it. "How is it that you are still in business, old friend? When people walk in the doors, they can't help but see my reception area with its big, broad doors and polished wood surfaces. However, in your case, one would need a professional tracker to find your gate area since it is so obscure and easily over-looked. What is remarkable is that your own father built this airport, and this is all you have left of his work.

"Think of it; this was once yours, but now it is nearly all mine. I have expanded my footprint in this facility so much that most people don't even know you exist. You and your airline are a relic of the past, but I will continue to grow my brand and domain and move boldly into the future. But sadly, you and your hopelessly irrelevant airline will one day vanish."

The pilot finally spoke. His voice was clear, confident, and unshakable, as if he was listening to the boastful claims of an ignorant little child. "Yes, Reinhard, you have a massive presence in the airport that my father built. However, you managed to get all of this through deception and fraud. You have bribed government officials, promised your customers something you can never deliver, and callously sent your passengers to a destination that is only a cruel hoax. Furthermore, you are guilty of racketeering, assault on my workers, and murder of many who have been faithful to me.

"You have perpetrated every criminal offense there is to get what you believe you now have. But the truth is, you own nothing here, for you are merely an unlawful squatter occupying a place that does not belong to you and that you will never possess for your own. One day, Reinhard, you'll be bankrupt, and when all your corruption has been exposed, you will be imprisoned on the very island you have deceitfully called Paradisum."

Mr. von Lux-Ferre smiled at him and said, "You have a very vivid imagination. This empire of mine will never fall. As you can see, I am too big to fail. And what you call corruption, I call creatively competitive business practices. I'm here to stay, and you are on your way out, old friend. I provide an essential service to people that want to find rest and be rewarded for a life of toil and hard work. I am flying the masses to Paradisum, and business has never been better."

"Why don't you tell Derek here the real name of the island where these people are headed to, Reinhard?"

Rolling his eyes, he offered, "Why, it's Paradisum, of course. To suggest otherwise insults common sense and my unimpeachable integrity."

Quietly, the pilot asked a question, but in doing so, he sounded like a prosecutor in a courtroom, "Paradisum is the name you have labeled it on your navigational charts and slick advertisements. It has a more ancient name, does it not?"

The CEO shrugged his massive shoulders and replied, "I have no idea; I was never very good at remembering archaic and irrelevant historical trivia."

While the pilot looked at Mr. von Lux-Ferre, his words were directed at Derek as if he were now the jury, "Tartarus is its old and original name, and it is the island that the Wide-Open Skies flights go to. Paradisum is my island and belongs to my family. I am the only one who knows how to get there, and I only take those willing to let me fly them there under the conditions I have set. The entire Wide-Open Skies operation is based on a fabrication, a lie of promising something it could never deliver."

Mr. von Lux-Ferre laughed at these comments. He looked at Derek and said, "Sad, isn't it, Derek? This sounds like sour grapes, and the ravings of a failed businessman watching his market share dwindle and his beloved company fall into ruin."

Derek felt insignificant amid this conflict between two mighty foes, but he did have a question which he addressed to Mr. von Lux-Ferre, "Is it true about there being two islands?"

The giant man looked down on Derek, smiled, and smoothly said, "Derek, this is a very complicated and, dare I say, cloudy piece of history that this man and I have between us. So, it is not a simple answer of yes or no. Yes, it's true, I once worked for this man, but now I hope it is clear to you why I started my own company. I admit that from time to time, I have been forced to use creative and somewhat uncultured methods to grow this empire, but I assure you that it was all in the interest of serving the public.

"I would not have employed such means if I wasn't mistreated and left with no other options. However, regardless of how distasteful those methods were, it is plain to see that the end has more than justified the means I was compelled to use. So, today, people who fly on our airline love and appreciate what I am offering them."

"So, are there two islands or not?" This time Derek spoke more emphatically and with a hint of irritation.

"Patience, I was coming to that part. To address your question directly, as for there being two islands, but one is a ruse, as it has been alleged, that is both true and false. I will acknowledge that I was removed from his island due to his anger and jealousy, but I have found another one, an even nicer one to send our customers to.

"So, yes, there are two islands, but mine is also a paradise. And since this man is obviously not a strategic thinker and clearly not very good at business, he was not wise enough to copyright the name 'Paradisum' all those years ago. Thus, I have every right to call the new island Paradisum as well." The CEO looked squarely into the eyes of the pilot and spat the words, "So, sue me."

Unfazed by the insults and demeaning nature of Mr. von Lux-Ferre, the pilot replied, "You can call a serpent a dove because you find it up in a tree, but it doesn't change the fact that the slimy creature is cursed to slither along in the dirt and will never know the freedom of flight. That island you now call Paradisum is a cursed and horrible place; changing its name does not change its nature."

At this comment, Derek heard the CEO make a guttural sound as if groaning or growling, but he could not tell which. Regardless, the big man bristled with displeasure.

The pilot pressed more, "If your island is so wonderful, why have you never been there yourself? You and I both know that what you call a relaxing vacation spot is a barren and isolated rock that no one would willingly choose to go to if they knew the truth."

The CEO recovered somewhat and offered, "Now, I make no secret that I have never been there because I have a very successful business to run. I have important matters to attend to, and I can't do those things if I am flitting back and forth between my headquarters and the island; that is why I have recruited and trained my own pilots. As for your negative characterization of the new island, it seems to me that you're engaging in a bit of mudslinging to keep people from going there and having a good time."

The pilot looked intensely at Mr. von Lux-Ferre, and his tone of voice caused the hair on Derek's arms to stand up. "Reinhard, on my word, I promise you that one day I will make sure you take a one-way flight to that infernal place. Then all those people there will greet you and demand to know why you tricked them into going to that desolate place."

Mr. von Lux-Ferre calmly smiled and shook his head. However, two things disturbed Derek. First, the confirmation that there was a second island, and it might not be as lovely as the original Paradisum. He pondered that if was lied to about that detail, what else was fiction? The second bothersome issue was that for all his calmness, confidence, and charm, a slight bit of sweat emerged on the upper lip of Mr. von Lux-Ferre, and his hands trembled as if terrified but was well trained to control and hide his fear.

In Derek's mind, something felt amiss here because, on the surface, Mr. von Lux-Ferre held all the cards and wielded absolute power, yet he seemed to be bluffing with nothing in his hands.

With a sad and dejected look, Mr. von Lux-Ferre slowly spoke to the pilot, "As always, you see me as an adversary, but all I ever wanted was what I was entitled to and a chance to establish my own name. For that, you exiled me. And today, you have wounded me deeply and made me look like a monster in the eyes of a potential client. With that, I must leave all of this unpleasantness behind and return to running a real airline. However, before I do, Derek, you, my good man, have a plane to catch, and we have a fine first-class seat reserved just for you. If you will accompany me, I will speed you on your journey in luxurious comfort and style."

Derek stood there and didn't know what to do.

Xi looked at him with pleading eyes and whispered, "Please, don't go with him."

The pilot looked at Derek and said, "Derek, if you want a flight to the true island of Paradisum, you must follow me. I make no promises of a pleasurable journey filled with all manner of delights. All I promise you is that I will get you to the island, which this untrustworthy person cannot do. I hope you will join me on today's flight." With that, the pilot turned and walked towards his company's gate.

The pilot knew Xi would continue his war with his former boss so he grabbed him by the arm and said, "Let's go, Xi. There are many more exciting battles ahead for you, but this is Derek's decision, and he has to make up his own mind about which island he wants to go to." As Xi was half pulled along, he looked back

at Derek with concern and at Mr. von Lux-Ferre with
deepest loathing.

12

The Offer

Mr. von Lux-Ferre walked up to Derek, reached out with a cadaverous hand, and grabbed his forearm. From just a few feet away, he seemed young and strong, but up close, he appeared to be ancient, leathery, and haggard. No matter his age, he had an unusually strong iron grip. Derek tried to recoil gently, but the grasp of the white-suited man was locked down hard. It was like he was pulling against a locomotive.

"Why don't we take a walk? First, let me apologize for that bit of distasteful behavior. I am always a gentleman but also a man of deep passion. One of my few faults is that I don't handle senseless recalcitrance very well. You see, I have done my best to help that pilot fellow, and he has rejected my decency and courteousness.

"When I saw that he was falling on hard times, I even offered to buy him out so long as he would be willing to give me my due respect. I even promised him that he could run the entire company if he would give a simple acknowledgment that I was his superior. He has stubbornly refused my generosity, and when such ill-mannered behavior happens, even the most well-natured of gentlemen can stumble into the occasional public display of incivility.

"I am guilty of being pushed into rudeness, and I hold myself at fault for allowing this man's lack of good judgment to cause me to speak in such a harsh fashion. That was something that no customer should ever have to witness, and I ask for your forbearance on that matter." The panache of Mr. von Lux-Ferre's demeanor had returned in full bloom, and he was back at the top of his game as a gentleman and an orator.

As they slowly walked with the CEO irresistibly pulling the smaller man along, the conversation continued, "Derek, I know you are a wise man, and I want you to be sensible about what is in front of you. It would pain me to see you act like that poor pilot and miss out on an outstanding proposition for the offer of a lifetime that has fallen into your lap. If I have judged you correctly, as the discerning man I believe you to be, then I think you know the smart play here. I will personally walk you through the ticketing and boarding processes and ensure that you are treated with the best service that our company has to offer."

Derek stopped in midstride and with an act of sheer will and determination, he broke free from the vicelike death grip the other man had on him.

"Wait a second, Mr. von Lust or whatever your name is! I'm having difficulty remembering things and need a second to think."

The CEO gave a pleasant smile, but a hint of irritability arose in his smooth voice, "Of course, and please call me Reinhard; after all, we're friends."

Derek breathed heavily, "No, no, we are not friends. I just met you, and in this short amount of time, you have not been honest with me, and now you are trying to drag me into making a choice I may regret!"

"I assure you that I would never want you to make an ill-conceived and uniformed choice."

"But you hid the truth about the whole situation, especially the fact that there is more than one island."

The giant man sort of cocked his head to one side and, in an impassioned plea, replied, "Derek, if we are not friends, then we certainly should be friends, for you can trust me, and furthermore, why would I hide the truth from you?"

"Maybe you're just a crass businessman who has no idea what truth is."

"Since you have brought up this notion of 'truth,' I would like to quote a famous line that seems to apply, 'You will find many of the truths we cling to depend greatly on our own point of view.' So, in this case, that infuriatingly stubborn pilot says that his island is wonderful, beautiful, and exclusive, but from my point of view, the island I send people to is equally, if not more, lovely. After all, what is truth but just our individual points of view?"

Derek's chest heaved as he tried to clear the fog that had settled in his mind, "Well, one truth is that your passengers, all of your employees, and even your paid lackey, Dr. Martov, believe there is just one island when there are in fact two separate islands. They were lied to as to the real situation! Why would you hide that truth from the people you say you serve and work for you?"

Mr. von Lux-Ferre dropped his head and looked pensive for a moment, "Derek, you must remember that running a business is about making decisions, important decisions, and sometimes tough decisions which only one person can bear the responsibility for, and in this case, that is me. Some types of information are corporate secrets, and as such, a justifiable level of discretion must be maintained. If not, then the revelation of this information could cause confusion and anxiety in the public's minds and give our competitors an unfair advantage in business.

"I am the last person who would ever want to deceive another creature. So I had to go against my own honest nature and make the hardest decision of my career: to keep this issue of two islands hidden from the public and, unfortunately, from even my devoted employees.

Can you imagine the chaos, not to mention the loss of market share, that would happen if that corporate secret got out? The public would be outraged, and they might even consider flying on a less capable and more dangerous carrier like the one my former boss founded and that imbecile Xi now works for. If that were to happen and a disaster occurred in which people were hurt, then I would never be able to forgive myself.

"In this case, I embraced the distasteful notion that honesty is often irrelevant; public safety is what I had to focus on. I beg you to understand that. I have learned that honesty has its place. Still, it is a bit overrated in business anyway, and this mania, for absolute truth, is, in my opinion, foolish and bad for business. That sort of dangerous legalism keeps us from making the right decisions and doing the things that are for the greater good.

"My deepest desire is only for the flying public to arrive safely at my island and that we put out of business those airlines that either can't or refuse to keep up with the times and ask the public to take unnecessary risks." As the CEO finished, his face had the appearance of a man who had poured out his soul and made an extremely painful personal confession.

"Thank you, Reinhard, that was a very heartfelt and moving speech." The CEO pleasantly smiled, but then Derek, whose thinking grew clearer by the moment, quickly continued, "It's a little too well rehearsed, though. You've made yourself out to be the victim here and a crusader who fights for the little guy. I'm sorry, but I have a hard time buying all of this."

Derek paused and let those words sink in. The tall CEO seemed a bit taller suddenly, as if it were a trick or optical illusion designed to intimidate Derek.

He felt an infusion of courage and said, "If you love this island of yours so much, then why haven't you been there?"

The corporate giant snapped, "Oh, are we back to that again?" Derek could see the anger swell in Mr. von Lux-Ferre's face. Just as the pilot seemed to bring light into the room when he entered, this man seemed to be sucking it in like a black hole. For an instant, his face became gnarled and vicious, and just as quickly, as if he realized he had dropped his guard, he was pleasant and congenial again.

"Derek, Derek, we are running out of time, so let's make a deal. I want to make you an offer that I have made to only a few people. Can we calmly sit down and politely discuss this without all this harshness? Just hear me out, please."

Warily, Derek agreed, and the two of them sat on a nearby bench while the two associates stood nearby. "Now, I am not saying you are, but let's say, just for argument's sake, that you will fly with us today. In exchange for your doing that, if for any reason you find the experience unpleasant, then I promise you we will refund the entire cost of your ticket, except for the typical administrative fees. Does that sound fair?"

Derek did not answer this offer, but the CEO ignored the silence.

"You have my personal guarantee that this flight will meet all your expectations or your money back; there is no way for you to lose! The only way it could be better is if it were free, which I can't do, by the way." A greedy and even hungry look appeared in Mr. von Lux-Ferre's eyes, like a dingo watching a child from the bushes.

Derek tried to remember his conversations and experiences from the day so he could make a thoughtful and reasonable decision. The hulking CEO leaned over, put an arm on his shoulder, and whispered, "Make the wise choice here, my friend, and just take the low-hanging fruit. Walk with me just a few steps to our ticket counter and all this silly drama will be over, and you will be off on the ride of your life.

"Think of it. Eating and drinking the finest the world has to offer, flying in comfort in the heart of that big, beautiful beast of an airplane that's just waiting out there like your own personal chariot, and being in first class where you belong and where you can be proud of who you are and the status you have achieved. What do you say, won't you taste the good life that you deserve?"

Derek stood up and left Mr. von Lux-Ferre sitting on the bench, and even then, the two men almost looked eye to eye. "Well, you have convinced me."

"Excellent choice, my friend; this will be a day you will long remember!" the CEO proclaimed, clapping his large, spindly hands together.

As the victorious CEO stood up to shake the smaller man's hand, Derek said, "Yes, you convinced me—to fly with the other airline. There is absolutely nothing that you said today that I trust. I think you are a very cunning businessman, but one who is full of lies. I think it would be a mistake to be one of your customers. Thank you for the time, but I have a flight to catch."

Like a dragon spreading its wings and growing to its full size before unleashing a fiery attack, the enormous man seemed to grow even larger. Perhaps it was his imagination, but to Derek, the CEO's size had actually increased and he was so prodigious that he could have straddled the entire concourse. His eyes narrowed to vicious-looking slits, and then like hot lava spewing forth, his angry words erupted, "You insolent little fool! How dare you turn me down! I offered you the best there is in life, and you treat me this way? You will regret this, you wretched little worm of a man!"

"I don't trust you, and I think you are a pathological liar. Goodbye."

Derek turned away and pushed his luggage cart quickly toward what now seemed like a sanctuary, the humble and almost hidden ticket counter where he had first met Charis. As he walked away, his legs sped up. He pictured himself running for the border of a free country, having escaped from a terrible prison camp. The angry predator behind him continued to spew forth vitriol and threats as thick as hail while his language grew more vile, filthy, and less polished as Derek walked on.

Out of nowhere, there was a flash and a flurry in the shape of a sprinting man who ran full speed at Derek. At first, he believed he was under attack and raised his arms to defend himself. However, he then recognized the charging face belonged to Xi as he grabbed him and gave him a giant bear hug. "Wow, that was close! I was so afraid you were going to go with that hobgoblin!"

"I almost did. In fact, I wanted to so bad, and if you hadn't told me to wait on that bench, he would have gotten me on his plane."

Xi pushed Derek toward the ticket counter, where a beaming Charis awaited him. As they walked, Xi turned around and walked in a way so he could see behind him. He glowered at the seething Mr. von Lux-Ferre as if he were a herd dog defending a lamb from a carnivorous beast.

As they locked eyes, Xi mouthed the words, "You may kill me one day, but today you lose!"

The CEO answered back, "Well, at least I have something to look forward to, and your head will make a fine trophy for the wall of our staff lounge." And with that, he skulked away.

13

The Baggage

While Xi and Charis were beside themselves with joy, they also knew one more hurdle remained for Derek to overcome before he could go through the gate and get on the flight: his luggage would be a problem.

The pilot stepped behind the desk and, in a matter-of-fact way, declared, "Derek, I want to welcome you on board; however, you must leave your luggage behind."

This statement puzzled Derek, but he thought there must be a simple explanation, so he asked, "I suppose it will be brought later on?" He remembered that both Xi and Dr. Martov had mentioned something about a peculiar issue with the luggage policy, and this must be it.

With a kind look, the pilot explained, "No, you must abandon your baggage here, for these things cannot come on the flight and would never be allowed on the island."

Stunned by this revelation, Derek stammered, "Well, I need to take my clothing with me; I mean, what will I wear on the journey and the island? Besides that, I also have some gourmet food and twenty-five-year-old single-malt scotch that I bought in the duty-free store. I can't just throw that stuff in the trash; it was insanely expensive!"

It dawned on him that the baggage policy was much more than a strange procedure that might cause a delay in receiving one's bags. No, this wasn't even close to what he had thought would be the requirements or limitations, and it seemed beyond the pale of irrationality. He was ready to fight this protocol and make demands. *Surely*, he thought, *there was some room here for reasonable negotiations.*

Derek looked across the ticket counter and realized this would be an uphill battle. The pilot shook his head ever so slightly and gravely said, "I realize this is difficult to hear, but eating, drinking, and impressing others with clothing are the sort of things that those poor souls on the Wide-Open Skies plane are concerned with to the point of obsession. They believe these are the indicators of true living, achievement, and what life is really all about. On the island of Paradisum, we aren't concerned about such things, for they have nothing to do with an authentic life. You cannot bring them, my friend."

This unexpected development clearly irritated Derek, but deep down, he also knew that these things were not worth missing the flight over. Reluctantly, he responded, "Fine, I'll ditch the clothes and leave the food and whisky behind if you insist. This all sounds really weird, but if that's the rules, then I guess I should abide by them."

The pilot looked at the baggage cart and asked, "Is all that clothing and duty-free items?" The pilot knew the answer, but he gave Derek the opportunity to be transparent and come clean.

"Well, no, there are some smaller items in a couple of bags that are special keepsakes, and I can't part with them."

The pilot looked quizzically at him and asked a follow-up question, "You *can't* part with them, or you *won't* part with them?"

Derek grew exasperated and, with pleading eyes, said, "Seriously, I would prefer not to lose them. They're precious to me, and some of those things were handed down through my family and are at the heart of my personality and individuality." He stood there moodily with a sullen and defiant look on his face. He hoped that by expressing his extreme displeasure, the pilot would understand and bend the rules just a little for him. This sort of game had worked for him many times in life, and although the tactic was manipulative, it usually allowed him to get his way.

The pilot remained as unyielding as a block of granite, "Derek, I have bad news. None of that can go on the plane with you. It is too burdensome, and there is no room for those things on my airplane."

Looking both forlorn and angry that his ploy didn't produced the desired result, he demanded, "I really must protest; this stuff is important, and I want to take it with me! I have a whole collection of rare books that I've grown fond of and that express my beliefs on philosophy and religion and are special to my cultural heritage. These books belonged to my father and grandfather before him, and they form the core of who I am. This is my identity, don't you understand? I think it is asking too much for me to give them up. They are going with me!"

The pilot looked with concern at Derek and said, "I am sure it is hard to part with things that you have such a deep personal attachment to, but unless you leave them behind, I will not let you go to the island. Those are the rules for all my passengers, and every piece of your baggage must stay behind. If you are to fly with me, then there are things you will have to lay aside. I know you think that is unfair, but it is not. I promise you that everything you leave here will be replaced with better things when you get there. Besides, the good news is, on the island, we have the best books of all, and they will give you the best picture of philosophy, religion, and the sort of culture that is acceptable."

He thought he may have made a big mistake and glanced back toward the Wide-Open Skies ticket counter, but then he thought, *What am I doing? I can part with these books. I'm just being sentimental and trying to hold on to things I should have given up years ago.*

Resigned to his situation and with gritted teeth, he muttered, "Fine, it can all stay, but I still think this is a lot to ask of a passenger." Derek had a growing emptiness as he contemplated his losses, but at the same time, he felt lighter and free, not having all that extra stuff to keep up with.

The pilot looked deeply into Derek's eyes and said, "I understand what it means to make sacrifices and to leave things behind. I gave up a great deal to keep this air route open for people to come to Paradisum, but it has all been worth it."

Derek reached down and grabbed a small carry-on bag, and said, "Can I go through now?"

The pilot looked down at the bag and again shook his head, "No, you may not. Derek, while I admire your persistence, I think you mistakenly believe the rules don't apply to you. You believe there might be some trivial exceptions and things I will turn a blind eye to. As I said, there is absolutely no luggage allowed on this flight."

At this, Derek groaned. "That's ridiculous! I can hold this in my lap or put it under my seat. It weighs next to nothing and won't take up any room at all."

"Derek, let me ask you, just what do you have in the bag?"

At this query, Derek grew cryptic and even embarrassed, "Well, stuff."

The patient aviator softly responded, "Naturally, I had assumed it was 'stuff.' Why, no one would be silly enough to take an empty bag on the plane. Now, specifically, what sort of stuff are we talking about?" the pilot probed.

Derek stammered and searched for an answer, "It's personal."

His evasiveness brought a perceptible hardening in the pilot's face. With an unblinking stare that was as pitiless as the sun, the pilot looked at Derek. He was unable to look back into this face. Without looking up and breathing hard, he murmured, "They're my most private things that belong only to me. They're mine alone to enjoy and indulge in when I want. They aren't harmful, and I never use them to excess. Frankly, I see this as an incredibly serious invasion of my privacy, and I think it is offensive to put me on the spot like this."

The pilot grimaced and slowly spoke, "Listen, I know I am asking a lot from you, but if you fly on my plane and journey out to my island, then you must abide by my rules. Those who don't follow my instructions are not allowed on board my airplane; it's as simple as that." Although quietly spoken, the pilot's emphasis on the word "my" was like the reverberation of a sledge-hammer in Derek's mind.

The pilot let that last statement hang in the air for a moment before he continued, "The things in that bag would cause you to be an outcast on the island, and by your holding on to them, it would prove that you truly don't belong there. If you are unwilling to give these items up, then what you are saying is that you don't trust me to take care of you and provide for you on this flight and when you get to our destination.

"Call this a test of faith if you like, but this is what I ask of every passenger, and no one is exempt. My standards are absolute and nonnegotiable." The words were firm but gentle, like an iron hand in a buttery-soft leather glove. It became clear to Derek that he could not win this battle, and he had spent all of his resistance on someone he could not resist.

With kind eyes and a tender voice, the pilot spoke, "My friend, it's your choice. I won't force you to give up anything. If you want to keep your special things and indulge in your secret pleasures, I won't stop you. I respect your right to choose, but if you are unwilling to give up everything, I will sadly leave you here, and you must travel to the other island."

An awkward silence hovered at the desk, and slowly, Derek loosened his grip on the bag and let it drop to the floor. He was a man who was almost clean and nearly free of a burden, but not quite.

The pilot stroked his bearded chin with a gloved hand, and with a piercing look, he asked, "Is that everything?"

With a hesitant nod, he replied, "I, I think so." Derek didn't want to look at those eyes because he felt they could see inside his mind and read his very thoughts. He imagined that if he avoided looking directly at them, then the pilot would not know the truth.

Then, with a tone of voice that radiated neither anger nor friendliness but resonated with profound power and deadly authority, he spoke, "Are—you—sure?"

Something deep inside Derek told him there was a significant and abiding danger in this moment, and his next actions could have horrific and irreversible consequences. Still, he wanted to hide and not answer. In his mind, he wrestled with whether this man was a predator, which he needed to camouflage himself from, or a true friend.

Deep down, Derek knew he was caught by a person who could never be fooled or outsmarted. But was this man a carnivorous beast who hunted him and he must hide in the bushes for safety, or was he someone who genuinely wanted to help him? His choice boiled down to either surrender or walk away. It was now a matter of trust.

He took another step forward, though it took everything in him to act. Derek looked sheepishly at the floor, slowly reached into his coat pocket and pulled out a clear plastic bag with a few small bottles inside. He looked up and pled his case like a child begging to keep a candy bar in a grocery store checkout aisle.

"Please, these are nothing; each bottle has less than three ounces of fluid and would easily pass through security! One is a bit of tonic for my nerves, and this other one I only take sips of it when I want to forget my problems. My using these doesn't do anyone any harm."

The pilot gave neither admonishment nor encouragement, only a patient stare. Derek knew it was a lost cause. He removed two of the bottles from the bag and set them on the desk. With the skill of a polished magician, he quickly palmed the last one and hid it within a tightly closed fist. The pilot scooped the two bottles up and dropped them in a trash receptacle.

The pilot looked with very patient but steely eyes and once again confronted him, "There's one more bottle, Derek. Why are you trying to hide it? It cannot go with you. Even for this small token of your old life, I will leave you behind if you will not part with it."

The look on Derek's face first showed hurt but then quickly turned to vicious defiance. With boiling anger, he spat his words out, "It's just a bottle of cologne I bought in the duty-free area; what's the big deal? Look, this is Préférence Sensuelle Forte Eau de Parfum; it comes from Paris and is extremely expensive! I like how it makes me smell, and it's very popular with my generation. All the important influencers are wearing it."

The pilot smiled and said, "Yes, it is very much in vogue these days and is also extremely flammable. That for sure cannot go."

Derek stood dead still with a furious look on his face. His hand clenched the small bottle with a tenacious grip as if he were a drowning man holding onto a lifeline. He had bargained his way down to the point that this one item was all that remained of his self-will and identity. He seethed at the boldness of this man to ask him to give up every little bit of his life. It was unreasonable and unfair! This belonged to him and him alone, and he would keep it no matter the cost!

Then he looked down at his tightly clenched fist, and his fingers suddenly looked spectral, bony, and shriveled like the hands of Reinhard von Lux-Ferre. Derek recoiled at the appearance of his hand, and it so frightened him that he dropped the bottle, which shattered on the polished floor. The escaping aroma was no longer pleasant and sensual but wretched, and a small cloud of putrid green smoke wafted up from the sizzling liquid that scorched the floor. He leaped back and yelled, "What was in that bottle?"

The pilot tersely and calmly replied, "Death. That sweet-smelling toxin would have eventually taken your life and would have kept you from going to Paradisum. It is the same for anything passengers are unwilling to give up and feel they must hold on to. The things they refuse to give up in exchange for the island will eventually distort and warp their personhood and character. They inevitably end up like that sad man over there." The pilot pointed as he said this.

Derek turned to look where the pilot pointed, and he saw the Wide-Open Skies area. The boarding process had ended and the staff polished the big broad doors, removing all the fingerprints and traces of the people locked in the massive plane. They had to be ready when the next group of passengers arrived. He then saw a looming figure that leaned against the desk and looked his way. Reinhard von Lux-Ferre glowered at him, his malicious eyes held Derek in a state of paralysis, and he could neither move nor stop looking at him.

The spell broke when the pilot's calm voice asked, "What do you think, Derek? Can I put your name on our flight manifest? If you say yes, you will have to leave all this baggage behind and follow my explicit instructions during the flight. You will need to assist the other passengers and meet any needs that they have. Can you do that?"

Derek looked at him with exhausted eyes and said, "But you are asking so much of me."

The pilot looked compassionately at the trembling man and said, "That's right, I am asking you to give up everything to gain so much more. Trust in me, I won't let you down."

As he stood there and contemplated the requirements to fly and the troubling notion that he would have to leave all his valuables behind, he looked at Mr. von Lux-Ferre. In the most beautiful baritone voice, he called out to Derek. His voice floated on the air, intoxicating and hypnotic.

"My friend, I am sorry for my angry outburst before; I hope the heat of our disagreement has cooled. A gentleman should always be ready to make amends for the sake of helping others. I hope we can agree to let all of that be in the past. It's not too late for you to board our waiting aircraft! We will make your journey easy and pleasurable.

"Besides, we don't have a luggage limit; you can bring anything and everything you want with you! I promise you that we will never ask you to leave anything behind, nor will we check the contents of your luggage, for that would be intrusive, rude, and none of our business. Forget about all those silly rules and come enjoy yourself. I beg you as a friend; won't you please reconsider?"

Derek turned his back on the man in the white suit, also on the mound of luggage that was loaded on his baggage cart, and then he looked into the pilot's eyes. There he saw absolute truth and an ocean of compassion in those fathomless dark orbs.

He then turned to Charis, who simply whispered, "Just say yes."

He glanced over at Xi, who stood to one side with his eyes closed.

Derek shifted his gaze back to the pilot and surrendered, "OK, I'm in your hands." The pilot gave a smile that made the room so luminous that Mr. von Lux-Ferre's fine white suit looked like a dirty burlap sack in comparison.

Then he asked, "How much for a ticket to your island of Paradisum?"

Then the pilot, in a voice filled with joy and passion that made Mr. von Lux-Ferre's voice sound like fingernails on a chalkboard, said, "Well, my friend, that's the best part. It's absolutely free, and when you get to the island, everything there is yours to freely enjoy. And now, since you trust my promise to get you to the island, my good friend Charis will bring you through the gate. I will write your name on my flight manifest, which should do for this flight."

He walked around the desk and met the gate agent, who walked with him. Charis helped him through the narrow gate at the jetway entrance and then walked with him down the corridor. He felt like someone who had dreamed a terrible dream and had awoken to a beautiful reality of freedom and peace.

When they came to the ladder at the end of the jetway, Charis said to him, "It was my pleasure to serve as your gate agent today. You made the right choice in flying with us, and you will be forever glad you said yes. I will see you on the island one day when my shift here is finished. Until then, farewell and have a pleasant flight."

"Thank you for not giving up on me, Charis. I hope to see you soon."

14

Boarding

As Derek climbed down the jetway ladder, he heard the whine of the massive engines on the Wide-Open Skies jet as they spooled up. The boarding doors were shut, the jetway was pulled back, and those souls on board were irrevocably committed to that flight. A tug pushed the giant jet backward as the ground staff walked with the aircraft. He stood there and watched this graceful ballet of efficiency and power. The ground crew unhooked the tug, and when it had moved out of the way, the lumbering leviathan proceeded onto the taxiway slowly and almost effortlessly.

Derek glanced up to the same windows he first looked out of to see the two aircraft at the start of this very long day. So much had changed since he looked out those windows and laughed at the scene below. He was a different man who was no longer cynical about the small plane and the humble pilot. The little aircraft was now his plane, and the pilot who rescued him from the plotting of the diabolical CEO was now his pilot, and he felt a peace about this change that he could not understand. As he contemplated the shift his life had taken, a large, ominous figure walked up to the windows. Mr. von Lux-Ferre stood there and stared at him. He had a deep-furrowed scowl on his face. They briefly locked eyes, and after a moment, the large man turned and walked away.

From inside the cockpit of the tiny plane, Derek heard the radio traffic between the Wide-Open Skies pilot and the control tower. One of the voices on the radio belonged to the celebrity pilot J. Scott Wolfe. He was the pilot in command, and in a slight Southern accent, Derek heard him say, "Hello, tower, this is Wide-Open Skies flight 1989, ready for departure."

After he received runway instructions and takeoff clearance, the charming pilot radioed back, "Roger tower, depart on runway 256 and turn back to the east. Thank you, tower, and y'all have a blessed and prosperous day."

Derek walked up to the humble aircraft, where a door stood open for him to climb in. Xi waited for him beside the plane. In the distance, they both heard the roar of the WOS aircraft as the pilot shoved the throttles forward to takeoff power, and it started its roll down the runway. As the aircraft thundered forward and gained speed, it rotated off the runway and rose gracefully and smoothly into the air. Quickly, as the plane gained altitude, it made its departure turn and disappeared into a cloud bank and vanished from sight.

Xi put a hand on Derek's shoulder and said, "Hop in and let me help you get strapped in. You'll need to buckle up because it could be a bumpy ride."

Jokingly, Derek asked Xi, "Am I in the first-class section?"

As he said this, Xi's face broke into a broad grin, and he said, "It's all first class; now enjoy the flight, and I will see you someday on the island."

After Xi finished helping him with the seatbelt, he extended his hand, and after a firm handshake, the young man turned and walked back to the jetway area. Derek quickly looked around the cabin and counted four other passengers beside himself.

He also noticed that the pilot stood on the other side of the aircraft and leaned against the wing. He, too, had watched the Wide-Open Skies jet take off and continued to stare at the place in the clouds where it had disappeared. Derek noticed that the pilot lifted a gloved hand to his cheek and wiped away the tears that had trickled down his face.

When the other aircraft's sound faded, the pilot walked to the aircraft, opened the hatch to the cockpit seat, and climbed in. Before he put on his headset, he turned around to face his passengers. "This is going to be an adventuresome flight. Some of you have already lived a grand adventure in service to me, and now the island is your reward. For others, you just barely made it on the flight, but because of your faith in me as your pilot, you are welcome on the island just as the others are."

The pilot smiled and said, "Now, let me greet each of you properly and as members of my family."

The old man who had boarded earlier sat right behind the pilot, and he shook and appeared nervous. The pilot smiled at him, touched his trembling knee, and said, "Be at peace, my old friend. Just think, soon you will see your family members who are already on the island, and they will be waiting to greet you when we land. William, surely you are not nervous about flying, are you?"

The elderly gentleman bowed his head and, in a trembling voice, replied, "Sir, it's not the flight that I am nervous about. In fact, I wish I could fly this plane myself, but I know my piloting days are behind me. No, I'm just nervous to see my family who are there. I am also particularly eager to see my buddies who flew with me in the war and I never saw again, but I know they are on the island." His voice shook with emotion.

The pilot addressed the passengers and said, "Ladies and gentlemen, this is William Rittenhouse. He was a fellow aviator many years ago. He fought courageously as a military pilot in one of the great wars on this planet.

During that conflict, his aircraft was shot down, and he was captured in the country of Romania."

A lady in the back of the plane gasped excitedly.

"This fearless man would break out of the prison camp he was assigned to, and at night, he would travel to other prison camps nearby. He would then sneak into the other camps to tell the captives there about me and the island that we are going to. Crazy, huh?" The pilot beamed at the courageous old warrior, "You were so brave."

"I was scared to death, but I knew those men needed to hear about you."

The pilot added, "His captors eventually found out about it and nearly killed him."

"My copilot, who was with me, was shot the night we were discovered." William had a far-off look in his eye as he said this.

The pilot considered the honorable old warrior for a moment and then said, "Fortunately, even in the ranks of those on the evil side of a war, there are often valiant and high-principled people, and the commandant of his prison camp was such a person. After hearing the story of how he was risking his life to tell others about how to come to my island, that enemy leader had him escorted to any prison camp that he wanted to go to so he could tell his fellow captives about me and my island. Well done, Bill, and thank you for your service to me and for your courage."

The old aviator simply said, "Just following your orders, sir."

The pilot sat up, looked over the other passengers, and remarked, "Did I hear a sound back there from someone from the country of Romania?"

A very modest and quiet lady lifted her hand but did not speak.

"I see you back there, Silvia." Silvia was too embarrassed to say anything except the Romanian word, "Pace."

"Oh, she seems timid, but you must remember that Romanians are some of the most passionate people you will ever meet, and they are unafraid to speak their minds. If you ever share a meal with them, prepare to eat some delicious food, have a lively conversation, and stay a long time. They make me laugh. Romanians are also very loyal, and Silvia Tărniceriu is one of the most loyal people I have ever known.

"Sweet friend, you have known terrible suffering because of your commitment to me. You see, folks, Silvia faced intense persecution when horrible people were in leadership in her country, yet she stayed faithful. She even went to prison because she believed in me and my island and wanted to tell others about the truth. I helped to get her free, and after her release, she continued to work for me and tell others about the island. I know your family will miss you as you leave them today. They will also miss your exceptional Romanian cooking, but they will see you again soon. It's a true pleasure to take you to the island today."

The pilot turned his head slightly to see the man who was seated just across the aisle from Silva. He paused as he locked eyes with a somewhat older man who had deep-set eyes, a square jaw, and his head was absent of hair except for some wisps of grey on the sides. He had an intelligent face and a mischievous smile, which suggested that he had a readiness for a good joke.

The pilot remarked, "Today's flight has quite an international flavor. Homayoun, what a blessing it is to see you. When you and your wife, Sara, were going through your darkest hours, I worked on your behalf to help you through those difficult days." The pilot pointed to the man and said, "My friends, this is Homayoun Zhaveh, and he is Persian. If you know Persians very well, then you know how incredibly smart they are, how they love a good joke, and that they are proud of their long and rich history. Persians are also very willing to endure great pain for what they believe in, and my friend Homayoun has suffered more than his fair share of pain.

"Because the government of his country is exceedingly evil and hates me, he and his friends often had to meet in private to talk about me and the island. He and his wife were caught and thrown into a horrible prison for attending these secret meetings. His dear wife Sara is still in that terrible place for her dedication to me, but perhaps she will be released soon."

The pilot then spoke to Homayoun in flawless Farsi, "باتشكر از فداداری شما در برابر نفرت."

Even though Derek knew no language except English, he remarkably understood this phrase perfectly: "Thank you for your faithfulness in the face of hatred."

Derek didn't know what sort of linguistic trick this was, so he remained quiet, although it was the most bizarre thing he had ever experienced.

The pilot then told the smiling man, "Welcome on board, and I know you will enjoy the flight and keep the other passengers entertained with some fantastic stories."

Homayoun stood and nearly hit his head on the low cabin ceiling, but he held his hand to his heart, bowed his head, and replied, "عزام رب من است ای برکتبخشیده." Derek also heard this translation in his head and had no difficulty understanding the words, "The honor is mine, oh Blessed One."

The pilot then addressed the woman who sat in the seat directly across the narrow aisle from Derek, "Why, Dr. Jefferson, I can't tell you what an honor it is to be taking you to Paradisum today." He noticed her ebony cheeks streaked with the salty residue of tears. "I know you had colleagues from medical school on the flight that just departed, and I know how hard you worked to convince them to join you on this trip. Mildred, my dear, sweet friend, I share your sadness, but where we are going, there will be no more tears, and your life's work is greatly valued."

He then addressed the other passengers, "Dr. Jefferson served as a wonderful physician who took an unpopular stand in her country about the importance of life. She was so irresistibly persuasive that she even changed the mind of her country's highest leader to protect the lives of those who were yet to be born. You used your towering intellect, your position of influence, and your charm and wit for my service, and I am grateful. Welcome on board."

He turned to Derek and smiled. "Derek, I must tell you that you were a challenge to get on board today. I sent one of my best people to fetch you, and he nearly got himself beaten to death just to get your attention. Fortunately for you, Mr. Shengmo is as clever as he is bold. He figured you were the curious type and that you would want to know what was really going on. That's why he allowed himself to take such rough treatment from the security staff. Xi would say that it was all worth it. I suspect he is like Job's horse because he loves the battle. However, it still hurts me to see him suffer.

"As for my former servant, Reinhard von Lux-Ferre, he nearly had you in his talons. He is not as wise and as much of a gentleman as he likes to boast that he is. Fortunately for you, he talks too much and thinks too highly of himself, which has always been his downfall. I knew I had a chance to win you over when he was forced to reveal to you that another island existed.

"At that moment, you reasoned and thought for yourself, which is the one thing that Reinhard and his army of public relations staff don't want people to do. They would rather you make an ill-informed choice and take the broad, easy path that doesn't require any rational thought or investigation of the truth. Thank you for believing in me and leaving behind everything you held dear. It will more than be replaced when we get to the island. You are most welcome on board, and I am pleased to take you to my island and my home, which is now yours."

As Derek looked around the cabin at his fellow passengers, he felt a sense of shame and could only look down at the aircraft floor. The pilot knew Derek struggled and gently probed, "Derek, I sense something is troubling you, my friend; what is it?"

Derek lifted his head and hot tears ran down his cheeks. "None of this makes any sense. Sir, I don't deserve to be on this flight with these courageous and honorable people. I haven't done anything for you except give you and Xi a very hard time today. I don't understand why you would want someone like me to come."

The pilot looked around the cabin and then spoke in a clear and warm voice, "I dare say that every passenger on this plane feels exactly the same way as you do, Derek. But understand, what you deserve has nothing to do with your being here with us today. I offer this service as a free gift to anyone willing to reject the silly and worthless things that Reinhard von Lux-Ferre and his airline have to offer and will instead trust and follow me. The sad truth is those who feel they deserve to go to the island would never dare to set foot on this airplane. Their high opinion of themselves causes them to book a ticket on another airline that goes to the other island."

The pilot leaned over and opened the cooler he had placed in the airplane earlier that day. He pulled out an old bottle and something wrapped in a cloth, and he turned back around to the passengers and said, "Now, everyone, I have some refreshments for you before our flight." He unwrapped the cloth, and the aroma of fresh bread filled the tiny cabin. He broke off a piece and gave some to each of the passengers. "Eat, my friends; this is for your nourishment. This bread will help you remember this day and all that was done to get you on this flight." It was the sweetest, most satisfying food Derek had ever tasted. He thought that even the cuisine from the Michelin-starred chef on the Wide-Open Skies plane would taste like rancid gruel compared to this.

Next, the pilot opened the bottle of wine and poured a small amount into some ancient glasses that had been stowed under the seat. "This is a symbol of our relationship and a reminder of all the pain I have suffered to provide this service for you." Derek drank the liquid, and at first, it was very bitter, but as it went down, it became sweet. It lifted his sadness and the effect made him feel alive and free. He thought the wine must have come from grapes from the most fertile region on the planet.

As he swallowed the liquid, it calmed his nerves, he no longer had any shame, and a strange feeling of courage and desire for adventure came over him. At that moment, he didn't care if they were going to fly through the biggest cyclonic maelstrom or by the nap-of-the-earth over the most treacherous mountain range, for he felt ready for what lay ahead.

15

Flight

The pilot stowed the rest of the bread and wine and put on his headset. He radioed to the tower that they were ready to depart. Xi ran out and removed the chocks from the tires. The pilot yelled, "Clear prop!" and warned Xi to get out of the way when the propeller started spinning. The engine roared to life, and after he checked a few instruments, he released the brake, eased the throttle in, and the small plane lurched forward. Charis stood out on the tarmac as well. She wore a headset and waved to the aircraft as they rolled towards the taxiway. Xi saluted the pilot and flashed a thumbs-up to Derek as they passed him by. Derek heard the pilot on the radio with the control tower.

"Tower, this is Avem de Paradiso flight 001 requesting clearance for takeoff. We have six souls on board, including the pilot."

"Thank you, tower; cleared to depart on runway 077 and then turn back to the west."

The aircraft turned onto the active runway and started its takeoff roll. As the plane gained momentum, Silvia sung a song about the island, and Homayoun instantly joined her. Mildred blended her beautiful voice with the others, and Bill clapped and sang. It was a mixture of Farsi, Romanian, and English, and Derek heard the voices and understood the languages perfectly. To his great surprise, although he had never sung this song, he knew it as if he had learned it as a child. He, too, sang this song about Paradisum and about the man who was flying them there.

The airplane bounced down the runway, quickly rose into the air, and left the earth behind. As they sang, Derek looked across at Mildred, who was radiant and had an unnatural peace about her. He glanced up at the old man, who looked strangely ageless and joyful in the light that came in the windows. Derek turned back to Silvia; the beautiful Romanian became the picture of joy. Homayoun would have danced if there had been room for him to stand up, but he was content to stay seated and sang loudly and with a passion that only a truly free man can sing with.

The pilot was the embodiment of calmness and control, for he flew the plane as straight and level as if it were on rails. As for Derek himself, he was never so invigorated and peacefully satisfied. He sang this new song and no longer thought about the Wide-Open Skies flight. He could not even remember his abandoned luggage and all the things he once considered precious. Neither could he see Mr. von Lux-Ferre's face nor remember the sound of his melodiously unctuous and suave voice. All those things were cleansed from his memory by the bread, the wine, and the song he sang with this fellowship in the sky. As he sang, his thoughts focused on the island paradise that lay ahead and felt grateful to the man who took him there.

Appendix

General Comments

This book is a Christian allegory and is in the style of my favorite book to read other than the Holy Scriptures, *The Pilgrim's Progress*, which is also an allegory of the Christian journey to salvation and discipleship. I also recommend reading C. S. Lewis's book, *The Pilgrim's Regress*, the story of his salvation in allegory form. The genre of allegory is often effective to communicate an idea by using subtlety and narrative. However, this style is limited to only depicting a certain level of reality. John Bunyan, in the closing poem of the first part of *The Pilgrim's Progress*, speaks to the fact of this limitation when he says:

Now, reader, I have told my dream to thee,
See if thou canst interpret it to me,
Or to thyself, or neighbor: but take heed
Of misinterpreting; for that, instead
Of doing good, will but thyself abuse:
By misinterpreting, evil ensues.
Take heed, also, that thou be not extreme
In playing with the outside of my dream;
Nor let my figure or similitude

Put thee into a laughter, or a feud.
Leave this for boys and fools; but as for thee,
Do thou the substance of my matter see.
Put by the curtains, look within my veil,
Turn up my metaphors, and do not fail.
There, if thou seekest them, such things thou'lt find
As will be helpful to an honest mind.
What of my dross thou findest there, be bold
To throw away, but yet preserve the gold.
What if my gold be wrapped up in ore?
None throw away the apple for the core:
But if thou shalt cast all away as vain,
I know not but 't will make me dream again.

If you are familiar with John Bunyan's work, perhaps you have noticed some elements in this book that are similar to his *The Pilgrim's Progress*. I drew some inspiration for various aspects from his work to pay homage to a book I am so indebted to for my own spiritual growth. Here are a few of the elements I reference:

- The casino Vanitas plays off of Bunyan's town of Vanity Fair. Initially, I called the casino Vanity Flair but thought better since it lacked subtlety and sounded a bit hokey.
- Mr. von Lux-Ferre's size and ability to straddle the concourse when Derek rejects his offer is rooted in the reference to Christian's battle with Apollyon when Bunyan writes, "Then Apollyon

straddled quite over the whole breadth of the way…"

- After Derek rejects offer, the CEO reveals his true character, reacts with extreme violence, and hurls threats and insults at Derek. In describing this, there is a line, "The angry predator behind him continued to belch forth vitriol and threats as thick as hail," which is like Bunyan's line, "Apollyon as fast made at him, throwing darts as thick as hail."

Leaving John Bunyan, I want to address some of the other elements of this small book. I did not want to be cryptic in my use of language, nor did I wish to be tediously obvious. I use a good deal of Latin in the names of things and people. For example, the names of the two aircraft are Latin phrases. The small plane is named Avem de Paradiso or "Bird of Paradise." The Wide-Open Skies aircraft is named "Virgo Spiritus Temporis" or "Maiden of the Spirt of the Age." One embraces the role of escorting people to paradise, and the other embraces the role of giving people an experience that is ever-changing and stays in line with worldly values.

Broad and narrow roads are images that are referenced throughout the book. Our Lord taught about these two ways when He delivered the Sermon on the Mount (Matthew 7:13–14). WOS has a wide-bodied jet, wide, comfortable seating areas, and a broad jetway. WOS is a comfortable airline to fly on, and they make travel very easy. As for Avem de Paradiso, their passengers must enter through a narrow entrance, into a narrow jetway, and onto a narrow aircraft with limited space. Their belongings will not fit through the door or even on the plane and, therefore, must be left in this world.

The luggage policy of the two airlines represents two differing perspectives on life. On WOS, baggage is not an issue; people may bring anything they like and are not challenged. Their possessions represent their love of this world and the various dogmas, beliefs, and cultural artifacts that are precious to them, and they refuse to lay down. To fly on the small plane, all luggage must be abandoned, which is symbolic of leaving behind our old beliefs, cultures, philosophies, and attachments if we are going to walk with Christ (1 John 2:15).

As Jesus said in the Sermon on the Mount, a person cannot serve two masters (Matthew 6:24). In this case, a passenger cannot fly on two airlines; they must choose one. He calls us to come and die and then to die daily. The world calls us to come and live all we can, for tomorrow we die. One policy focuses on this world, and the other is about looking for the world to come.

One of the weak areas or "plot holes" in the story is that the aircraft is representative in this story of death and passing on to the next life. This is due to an allegory's imperfect nature, for it would have been difficult to tell the story as the plane ride to the island as representative of the journey of salvation and discipleship. I chose to tell the story this way, knowing this is not the normal salvation/discipleship process.

People come to faith in Christ, walk through the narrow gate, and walk the straight path for the rest of their days as Christians. In this case, Derek would be like the thief on the cross who came to salvation at his death. It's an allegory, so I beg your indulgence and hope you will not feel I am unfaithful to the process of salvation and discipleship.

The Characters

Most of the characters of this allegory are either historical or have a basis in reality. I intended to challenge the reader to dig deeper into Christian and secular history and to grow in their faith by learning of the work and efforts of great Christians who have come before us. Some contemporary depictions of individual characters hit close to home in describing actual people. Still, they are mere representatives of a larger group and are a composite of several people from their particular category.

Derek

An everyman-type figure, his name is common but has a kinship with the word "derelict," which is the spiritual condition he is in when he starts the day. The name "Derek" is ancient (from the sixteenth century) and was adopted into English from the German language and is the shortened form of the name "Diederik." The name means people ruler or ruler of the tribe. I did not choose the name because of its meaning, because Derek does not lead anyone in the story, but instead, I chose it because of its long historical popularity.

As for the character himself, I left out as many identifying descriptors as possible, with two exceptions: gender and language. He is the least developed character of all, and that is by design. I hope readers can project onto him a backstory, personality, and physical characteristics from their imagination. Obviously, he is male, and there was no way of getting around gender. The language identifier only made sense since my primary audience is English readers/speakers. Since I chose not to describe him physically, give him a backstory, or refer to his age, I hoped he would fit into many categories.

Charis

The Greek word for "grace" is the word Charis. Grace is the outworking of God's love to others, especially when they do not deserve it. Derek did not deserve to be treated with kindness and gentleness due to his rudeness and lack of respect for the pilot and his airline. Charis poured out her goodwill on Derek even though he did not deserved it. She is not a doormat or a hopelessly incurable nice person, for when Derek insulted the pilot, she became quite fierce as his defender. She is both tenderhearted and unbending in her standards.

Grace is not some mushy form of sentimentality that people mistakenly believe our Lord displays. Yes, we are saved by grace, through faith, but grace is not extended to those who reject Christ or those who will not receive His forgiveness and submit to His Lordship. Grace is a double-edged sword, freely given to those who humbly accept it but absolutely denied to those unwilling to repent and walk the narrow road of following the Lord.

Captain J. Scott Wolfe—The Celebrity Pilot

In the Gospels and the New Testament letters, the warning to be aware of false teachers is everywhere. Nearly every Gospel and epistle has some sort of warning about false teachers or false believers in it. This was one of the major themes of Jesus, the apostles, and the early church: Be aware of those who either infiltrate the church unnoticed or leave our Lord's and the apostles' orthodox teachings and take heedless followers with them. As soon as the new covenant church was founded, this plague descended upon it. The character of J. Scott Wolfe is emblematic of this plague and the deceptiveness and destruction it can bring.

This narrative reveals that J. Scott Wolfe once worked for the pilot alongside Charis. The promise of wealth and fame seduced him, but he also found the stand the pilot took to be too negative and unpopular for him to bear. His last name is a bit of foreshadowing (maybe a bit too obvious), for he is leading people in the wrong way, as Jesus (John 10:12) and Paul (Acts 20:29) said would happen.

There are hints that he is on the side of the health and wealth (false) gospel movement that advocates the position that the Lord wants His people to be prosperous, to be healthy, and live their best lives in this world rather than to be holy, faithful, and ready to suffer the inevitable consequences of discipleship. This teaching is heresy and does not align with any instruction in the Gospels or the New Testament epistles. It is especially seductive to those who live in a wealthy society like the decadent West, where suffering for one's faith is foreign; pragmatism is a virtue, and achievement and bucket-list living are the highest goals.

Whether or not J. Scott is a faithful follower of the pilot is not discussed. Just like there are Christians who have been taken captive by Lucifer to do his will (2 Timothy 2:26), he might have drifted in his faith due to the promise of riches like Demas did (2 Timothy 4:10). He certainly is a false teacher. He may have become one even though he was a true follower, as Paul said could happen (Acts 20:30). He could also fit into the category that John (1 John 2:19) and Jude (Jude 4) describe as someone who only appeared to be a believer. Still, in time, their true character is manifest either through trials or temptation.

J. Scott Wolfe is a tragic character whom Charis cares a great deal for. Her sadness is personal because he has made a terrible choice, and that choice has ripple effects on a larger scale because he now works to take people down the broad road of destruction.

The WOS Gate Agents (Ms. Black and Mr. Brown)

These two characters are demonic, but I used two species of spider to fashion the nature of their character. The female is like Latrodectus or the black widow spider. She is very aggressive and territorial and quickly moves in for the kill. She has no subtlety about her and uses all her powers to capture her victim.

The male is modeled after Sicaridae or the brown recluse spider. He is more refined and less aggressive. This spider's bite is often overlooked due to the anesthetic nature of the venom. If he had been left alone, this agent might have gotten Derek in his web, but the aggressiveness of the black widow agent destroyed his hopes of a nice and easy capture and kill.

The Gambler

Bertrand is a composite character of several skeptics. The name comes from Bertrand Russell, a strident atheist from England in the early twentieth century. He was aggressive in his opposition to Christianity but was a well-received author and a celebrated philosopher. While his name and works inspired this character, he was not the only one. Others whom I drew elements of his character were Friedrich Nietzsche and Robert Ingersoll.

In the front of Ingersoll's book, *The Gods and Other Lectures*, is the quote, "Give me storms and tempest of thought and actions rather than the dead calm of ignorance and faith. Banish me from Eden when you will, but first, let me eat from the Tree of Knowledge." This sentiment is not very intelligent, especially since most Christians go through horrible trials and persecution for their faith. I reworked the quote to fit the character: "Give me the storms and tempest of a deck of cards and the roulette wheel rather than the dead calm of an airplane seat to an imaginary paradise. Banish me from the floor of Vanitas when you will, but first let me have a roll of the dice, for to gamble is the essence of life and death."

The heart of a skeptic is that of a gambler, a reckless spiritual high roller willing to risk it all on their ego and intellectualism. They are ready to bet everything on the notion that once death comes, there is nothing beyond this existence. For them, this life is about using power to gain what is desired, for power is everything. For a true skeptic like Nietzsche, morality is just a human construct designed to control people and deploy power.

There is no right and wrong for the true skeptic. This is the gamble they are willing to take; there is no island, no heaven or hell, no judgment or accountability whatsoever. Death is just a cessation of electrical impulses in a collection of organic compounds, which is called a human being. Deep down, I sense that most of them are terrified of being wrong but are too proud to admit that they may have misjudged the nature of eternity.

The Singer

Naturally, I had someone in mind when I developed her, but like other characters, she is a composite of several people—most of them are still living, and some are even still singing. One singer who inspired this character died in May of 2023. Sadly, she got her start in a small church where she sang hymns and was trained as a musician by people who loved the Gospel, but when success came, she abandoned the faith.

One of the personal aspects of this entertainer is her appearance of being in the crowd but simultaneously being isolated from the masses of people behind a screen of handlers and security people. She is the quintessential celebrity who once entertained small groups of people with a guitar and a barstool. She was underpaid until discovered and then rocketed to the top of societal popularity. In my mind, her backstory included an upbringing where she learned to play and sing music in a Christian setting (choir, praise team, small church band). Still, when popularity came, she quickly abandoned any ties to the Lord Jesus because serving Him and the world cannot be done.

This is a sad but all-too-true story in today's entertainment industry, where the church trains people in the arts and music only to have them abandon their faith when fame and fortune beckon. In the story, she secretly admires the pilot from afar but is too cowardly to take a stand and associate with him publicly. In short, she is ashamed of him because she is in love with the world. She has counted the cost of associating with him and decided that it would diminish her brand, hurt her public image, and ultimately, his demands are too much for her to bear.

Dr. J. Martov

This revolting character is typical of Marxists who demand that everything be equal for everyone but secretly crave special treatment for the elites or "architects" of a revolution. He was modeled after one of the chief proponents of the Russian Revolution, Julius Martov. He was in the upper echelon of the Marxist movement in Russia until he had a falling out with Lenin and Stalin. He was exiled to Germany, where he started a pro-Marxist newspaper. He died in exile in 1923 when he could not return to Russia because Stalin, who hated him, would not provide the money for his medical care and travel back to Russia.

The character in this story displays a great deal of typical Marxist hypocrisy. For example, like the fictional character Dr. Martov, Marxists say they are for the little person and true equality. However, they usually harbor secret bigoted tendencies and believe they are entitled to the good life and a higher standard of living because of their intellectualism and sacrifices for the revolution.

In this book, there is one phrase borrowed from Lenin when he advocated the destruction of the Russian Tsarist government. The slogan is from the year 1917, when Lenin, who was marooned in Switzerland (poor guy) due to the imperialist war, began writing *State and Revolution* (he finished this work in August–September 1917), and in keeping with the communist doctrine he proposes the dissolution of the state or its extinction. The slogan for this was: "the withering away of the state."

In this story, Martov advocates for the withering away of the exclusivity of the pilot's claims of service to the island and bringing all airlines under one umbrella. This concept, in this context, is not about political or even corporate merging but the tendency to deny the exclusive claims of Christ and the "tolerant" demand that Christianity merge with other religions in a pantheistic conglomerate.

Xi Shengmo

Xi ZiZhi was born in 1836 in China. He became a Confucius scholar and an opium addict until he became a Christian. The Holy Spirit delivered him from his addiction, and he learned the Word and became a mighty man of prayer. He changed his name to Xi Shengmo because "Shengmo" means "conqueror of demons" in his native language. He was an evangelist, hymn writer, and church planter. Xi had a powerful prayer ministry. He saw many people delivered from addiction and sin by the power of the Holy Spirit. Xi died in 1896 at the age of 60.

Reinhard von Lux-Ferre

Getting an accurate depiction of Lucifer is difficult because we don't know much about him. From Scripture, we know he is an ancient angelic being who, at one time, was a faithful servant of the Godhead. He has a long history and was a creation of the Lord as an angelic leader and associated with the music in heaven (Ezekiel 28:13). Eventually, he led a revolt against the Lord in his attempt to usurp Him and take his throne. Due to his fall, he is now a deceiver, liar, murderer, and an accuser of those who belong to Christ. Most importantly, he is a defeated being whose false reign will come to a fiery and ignominious conclusion.

The character of Reinhard von Lux-Ferre is an amalgamation of both the human and the demonic. I borrowed the name Reinhard from the archinfidel and murderous thug Reinhard Heydrich, a Nazi leader and principal architect of the Holocaust. He died after he was gunned down in Prague in 1942 by brave guerilla fighters who heroically sacrificed their lives to bring his bloodlust to an end. As for the name Lux-Ferre, that is an easy one. It is the Latin name for Lucifer, which means "light bearer," thus Lux for light and Ferre (pronounced fair-ay) for bearer. We are told in Holy Scripture that he often comes disguised as an angel of light (2 Corinthians 11:13–15).

I chose to use a description of Lucifer as being a larger person who dressed himself in all white except for his black tie. This reference comes from Bram Stoker's novel *Dracula*, where he writes about the main character in the following way, "He was dressed in a dark suit of clothes, which seemed to be either of English or American make, of a style that he had seen in pictures and described to me, and which were undoubtedly of a bygone fashion. He wore a large, round, black hat, a long black coat, and a pair of black trousers. He had black gloves on his hands, and a white, heavy scarf was draped around his neck. His appearance was very striking, and, as I drew near, he gave a sharp look at me as if to see under my skin."

I attempted to make him appear gentlemanly on the surface because there is a popular mythology about Lucifer that he is a true gentleman, as suggested by Dennis Wheatley, an English author who wrote about the occult and black magic. However, Lucifer is not a gentleman, but like his other masks (bearing light and being angelic), this is only a ploy to deceive. Our Lord tells us that Lucifer is a thief who has come to steal, kill, and destroy (John 10:10), which are not precisely the qualities of a gentleman. No matter his polished manners, sophisticated appearance, and gentlemanlike refinement, Lucifer is a parasitic killer with no room in his heart for anyone except himself.

The island of Tartarus, the island that von Lux-Ferre sends people to, derives its name from the Greek language. In Greek mythology, it is the place where the Titans and others are imprisoned and await judgment.

However, it is also the word used in the Greek New Testament for hell, as found in 2 Peter 2:4.

As for von Lux-Ferre never having been to the island, that lines up with proper theology in that Lucifer has never been in hell. There is popular but erroneous theology standardized by such works as Dante Alighieri's *Divine Comedy* and John Milton's poem "Paradise Lost". However, nothing in Scripture supports this viewpoint, and it is a gross misrepresentation of him as a ruler of hell who enjoys his time torturing the souls of the damned.

Lucifer does not want to be in hell. Instead, he inhabits the earth and sees it as his domain, but it is not. Lucifer owns nothing or has the title to any property, such as the earth. Sadly, there are many teachers of this erroneous theology that is popular today. They suggest that he was given the title deed to the earth when Adam and Eve fell. This is untrue and against God's Word. This error results from people adding to the Word of God rather than searching the Scriptures and letting God's Word govern and limit their imagination. Satan is a usurper and a parasitic trespasser, but he is not an owner.

The Pilot

He's Jesus. I suppose I need to give more information than that. The poet W. H. Auden said, "It is impossible to represent Christ on the stage. If he is made dramatically interesting, he ceases to be Christ and becomes Hercules." I knew the pilot would have to represent the

Lord, but I wanted to ensure that I did not add anything or remove anything from Him or His character, as seen in Holy Scripture. I trod very carefully to ensure He was represented in the most biblically accurate way possible.

I did not want a Hercules, nor did I want a weak apparition. I studied the Sermon on the Mount for weeks to form the basis of the pilot character. In that sermon, we see Jesus as a teacher, as Lord, as authoritative, as compassionate, as Judge, and as King. He shows compassion, and He lays down some hard and immutable Kingdom principles that are beautiful, loving, and non-negotiable. Most people say they love the Sermon on the Mount, but I am convinced they have never read all of it, for if they had, they would either reject it because it is out of step with who they are, or they would change their ways.

I used the pilot motif because many people see Jesus as a "copilot," but that is a mistaken belief. Either He is the pilot, or He is not in the plane. Following Christ is about total surrender. The concept of luggage as an illustration was to show our Lord's demands for us to be His disciples without reservations or worldly attachments. Unfortunately, we often want to hold on to our old lives and pleasures, even if it means being exempted from heaven.

We mistakenly believe we can tote a lot of baggage into our walk with Christ. Incredibly, we try to keep our philosophies, ignorant forms of religion, rights, pleasures, secret vices, and worldliness that weigh us down and expect the Lord to accept us—He does not. While we may come to Jesus just as we are, His whole intention is to change us, for we cannot stay as we are and follow Him.

The Passengers

The four passengers are real people of great courage and accomplishment. I wanted to find inspirational people of courage and deep faith in the Lord Jesus. I am fascinated by people with stories of courage. I love to collect stories of courageous people such as Jacques Stosskopf, George Washington Carver, James Stockdale, Catherine Mary Ironside, Wilhelmina Helena Pauline Maria, Lord Nelson, Chester Nimitz, Alvin York, and on and on the list goes. I particularly love to read stories of courageous Christians who gave up their lives for the faith of our Lord Jesus. These people need to be highly esteemed in our Christian circles and studied. The Scripture tells us that the memory of the just is blessed (Proverbs 10:7), and we should endeavor to keep the memory of righteous people alive by telling their stories. I chose four people whose stories I have a great love for and who have made great sacrifices for our Lord.

Bill Rittenhouse

The story of William Rittenhouse is true. I met his widow, Nell, in Birmingham, Alabama, and had the joy of being her pastor. Bill wrote a book called *The Barbed*

Wire Preacher, and MGM made a short film about his World War II story in the 1950s. He became a pastor and founded a ministry that worked with NASA astronauts. During World War II, he was shot down over Romania and literally broke out of a prison camp to go to other camps to share the Gospel. His copilot was shot one night when they were caught (he survived), and Bill was brought before the camp commandant. When the Nazi officer heard the story of his secret ministry to the other camps, he provided a car and an escort to take him to any camp he wanted to visit so he could share the Gospel. Bill loved the Romanian people and helped to smuggle Bibles to them during the bleak years of Communism.

Dr. Mildred Jefferson

Mildred Jefferson became the first African American woman to graduate from Harvard Medical School and the first woman employed as a general surgeon at Boston University Medical Center. She was a remarkable person with an incredible mind. Dr. Jefferson, most importantly, was a fiercely committed Christian who was unyielding in her stand on the right to life for the unborn. She was so charismatic and persuasive that she is credited with changing President Ronald Reagan's view of abortion. She loved the Lord and served Him almost all her life. She became a Christian as a child in her hometown of Carthage, Texas.

Silvia Tărniceriu

This brave woman lived under communism in Romania during the dark days of the reign of Nicolae Ceaușescu. She grew up in a Christian home and stood for Christ when her teachers laughed at her and called her a fool for her love of Christ. She was a woman of deep faith. Prayer was the focus of her life, and the Lord answered her prayers. Even when imprisoned in Romania for not renouncing her faith, the Lord protected her and answered her prayers. After her release from prison and emigration to the West, she continued to serve the Lord and advocate for the persecuted Church.

Homayoun Zhaveh

Homayoun Zhaveh is the only living person of the four. He is from Iran, and he and his wife Sara were released from prison in May 2023. Their ordeal began in 2019 with their arrest when he and his wife were accused of secretly meeting with other believers while on vacation in the Caspian Sea region of Iran. They were both convicted and sentenced to nearly ten years in the horrible Evin prison in Tehran. He was (and still is) in poor health, and his prison sentence would have been a death sentence.

Even though the appeals process looked doubtful, in May 2023, an appeals court overturned their convictions and released them. The court found that being a Christian was not a crime, and it was natural for Christians to meet with others of their faith and to have books related to Christianity. Many people worldwide prayed for Homayoun and Sara, and God answered their prayers. Their horrible ordeal reminds us that living for Christ comes at a cost. For many Christians, that cost is their freedom and sometimes their lives.

About the Author

S tan Lewis is a pastor, author, and photographer whose love and calling is to help take the Gospel of Jesus to the four corners of the world. He previously published the books *Everyday Apologetics: A 100-Day Devotional Journey in Defending the Faith* (books 1 and 2) and *Unshaken: Grounding Your Faith for the College Journey*. He loves aviation and has flown on many different aircraft types in the military and as a civilian, and in his college days, he was a licensed pilot. He is a fifth-generation native of Pensacola, Florida. While he enjoys the natural beauty of the Gulf Coast, he relishes the cool air of the mountains of the western United States and Nepal. Stan and his wife, Kristin, continue to live in Florida and have raised three beautiful daughters. They are passionate boosters for the University of West Florida women's volleyball team. Stan has also been adopted by a feral cat named Goose—which is, of course, a female.

A free ebook edition is available with the purchase of this book.

To claim your free ebook edition:

1. Visit MorganJamesBOGO.com
2. Sign your name CLEARLY in the space
3. Complete the form and submit a photo of the entire copyright page
4. You or your friend can download the ebook to your preferred device

Morgan James
BOGO™

A **FREE** ebook edition is available for you
or a friend with the purchase of this print book.

CLEARLY SIGN YOUR NAME ABOVE

Instructions to claim your free ebook edition:
1. Visit MorganJamesBOGO.com
2. Sign your name CLEARLY in the space above
3. Complete the form and submit a photo
   of this entire page
4. You or your friend can download the ebook
   to your preferred device

Print & Digital Together Forever.

Snap a photo

Free ebook

Read anywhere

Printed in the USA
CPSIA information can be obtained
at www.ICGtesting.com
JSHW021100290824
69013JS00003B/48

9 781636 983776